FRIA
and the
CHRISTMAS DEVIL

A Novella

by Steven A. McKay

Also by Steven A. McKay:

THE FOREST LORD SERIES
Wolf's Head
The Wolf and the Raven
Rise of the Wolf

Knight of the Cross

For my mum.

Acknowledgements

As always, I've been helped a great deal when writing this novella. My early beta-readers Billy Moore, Yvonne McKay and Bernadette McDade gave me pointers on the very first draft. Robin Carter and Nicky Galliers then gave me some more detailed feedback and what you have here is the result.

Huge thanks to Phil Rose for writing the foreword – I've been a big fan of Robin of Sherwood for a number of years so to have one of the actors involved in my book...It is truly an honour and I'm still a little star-struck! My everlasting gratitude to Carole Elizabeth Ballard for setting it all up with Phil – she runs his official Facebook page which you should check out.

First though – warm some mulled wine, sit back, and enjoy our tale...

FOREWORD

Friar Tuck and the Christmas Devil – Tuck, Troubles and Trials

As I sit here with a Christmas tipple of mead in my hand reading Steven A. McKay's *Friar Tuck and the Christmas Devil* I remember my days as Friar Tuck in the very successful HTV production Robin of Sherwood, with Robin and Robert played by Michael Praed and Jason Connery respectively.

In fact, *Friar Tuck and the Christmas Devil* could well have been an episode in the series, as it successfully drew me back into the Tuck character and in my mind I was playing the bold friar all over again. Of course Tuck has had to do battle with demons before, as in the Robin of Sherwood episode, '*The Swords of Wayland*', where the famous Rula Lenska played Morgwyn of Ravenscar who tried to accumulate the 'Seven Swords of Wayland' in order to conjure the devil. The seventh sword was of course 'Albion', which was in Robin's possession.

Strange things happened during the filming of RoS. In one of the last shots of "The Swords of Wayland" Rula Lenska was hurrying across the causeway at St Michael's Mount in Cornwall. One of the production team looked up and realised there was going to be an eclipse! So the crew quickly changed from filming Rula, hurried to put a filter on the camera, and filmed the eclipse instead. In the episode, as she was running, it cuts to the eclipse, she screams, the moon turns blood red and...that was the end of her.

In the same episode the Merry Men, and Robin, were

bewitched and blinded. To do this, we were fitted with large opaque contact lenses that blocked our vision and made everything whiter. So none of us could see. At the end when we're pulling Robin – who was hurt – on a cart high up on a cliff the contact lenses made us so visually impaired that we kept heading too close to the edge.

The director kept shouting at us, to move left, move left – get away from the cliff! The lenses were awful and could only be worn for five or six minutes at a time, so filming took forever that day. What we do for our art...

Friar Tuck and the Christmas Devil is a cosy, hear-warming little story with a twist, and a pie of course, which is going to entertain adults and children alike. Perhaps best served by reading it all together, aloud, bringing back the old tradition of sitting around the fire at Christmas and telling the seaonsal tales as we did indeed do in times past and should do more often nowadays!

The tradition of story-telling cannot be more appropriate than at Christmas, when it's cold outside and we are huddled as families together.

So, curl up amidst your presents, good food, holly and ivy and all the traditional festivities and take time out from the hustle and bustle of Christmas mania to gather the family around, share time and enjoy this tale.

Invoke the myth and legend of Friar Tuck, and chomp into that pie as you listen to the story.

May I wish you a wonderful yuletide season, and all good cheer my 'little flowers'.

Phil Rose,
AKA Friar Tuck from Robin of Sherwood

https://www.facebook.com/groups/PR.FT.OFC/?fref=ts

BRANDESBURTON, NORTHERN
ENGLAND,
DECEMBER AD 1323

Holy Mary, Mother of God. It's him! The devil!

The man shrank back, too anxious to approach his own front door for fear of what terrors he might find inside the thatch-roofed hovel he called 'home'.

The snow had fallen sporadically for the past week or so and had been particularly heavy that day, leaving a clean white covering on the land. The roads around the village were, of course, muddy and sodden from travellers' feet and the wheels of delivery wagons and the animals that pulled them but here, outside the old peasant's home, the snow was thick and fresh and untouched.

Or at least it *should* have been untouched, since no one ever came to visit the man and, as his family had all died or grown-up and left to live elsewhere, there was really no reason for anyone to have been near his front door.

So the sight of footprints leading towards the threshold had made the peasant pause and then stare, wide-eyed and terror-stricken at the low dwelling, which had begun to seem horribly sinister in the early-evening gloom. For upon closer inspection the prints in the snow weren't normal human, or even animal prints – they appeared to have been made by some bipedal beast with hoofs for feet. Cloven hoofs.

"The devil!" the peasant shouted in alarm, his strangled cry somewhat muffled by the falling snow yet still loud enough to bring his neighbours to their own doors. Their faces peered out, framed in the orange glow from their cosy hearths.

"What's going on out there?" a voice demanded. "I'm trying to get my children abed, Ivor. What's all the shouting about?"

"The devil's been in my house!" the peasant cried in reply, shuffling backwards away from the haunted place, waving his arms towards the hoof prints in the snow. "Call out the tithing! Someone send to the city for the sheriff's men – the fiend might still be inside. Look at the marks it's left; the thing must be huge!"

People began to spill into the street at the noise. Men carried wooden clubs, pitchforks, longbows or whatever other weapons they owned; mothers tried to hold back their children who, frightened but excited, called to their friends, wide-eyed and smiling.

"James!" The old peasant spotted a work-mate of his, a big man, who was watching events from the safety of his own front door. "James! Fetch your dog – it'll chase out the devil for us. You people, be ready to defend yourselves when the foul beast is chased into the open."

The villagers seemed unwilling to come anywhere near his hovel, fear keeping even the biggest, hardest of the men at bay, although James had apparently gone to find his dog for his bulk had disappeared from his doorway. The big man came back a moment later with the hound on the end of a length of rope.

It was a big dog, its head almost as tall as its owner's waist, although it was lean and rangy, being used for hunting rather than fighting and the frightened Ivor wished one of his neighbours owned something more vicious like a mastiff. Even the devil wouldn't want to face one of that giant breed!

The common folk of Brandesburton had good reason to be jumpy and fearful; in the past few weeks there had been many strange happenings around the village. A number of people – stolid, trustworthy citizens – had reported thefts from their homes and workplaces. Even the presence of locked doors didn't seem to be able to stop the thieves yet the doors were never broken down – it was as if the locks had simply been bypassed somehow...

On a few occasions the burgled buildings had shown signs of similar, cloven hoofprints in the mud or snow outside and so, of course, the rumours started.

The gossips had come close to hysteria when the blacksmith, a dumpy man who made up for his lack of height with the biggest arms Ivor had ever seen, had been reduced to a quivering wreck when, he claimed, a horned, glowing demon had brushed by him as he opened the smithy one morning. Some of his best pieces were missing and, as usual, hoofprints were found tracked along the entrance to the building.

Since then more people had come forward telling tales of sighting the devil, be-horned and with eyes that burned red like hellfire, leaping from rooftop to rooftop and howling with insane laughter.

Ivor knew some of those witnesses and he knew they wouldn't lie. If they said they'd seen Satan in Brandesburton it had to be true – who would lie about something like that at this time of year, when folk were preparing to celebrate the birth of Christ?

And now the devil was in his own house! The peasant clasped his hands and shakily mumbled the Ave Maria and Pater Noster as James led the big harrier towards the hoofprints in the snow.

The front door to the dwelling was slightly ajar although, as usual with these recent break-ins, it hadn't been broken off its hinges or had the lock smashed, and the dog approached, apparently interested more in pissing all over the fresh white snow than in chasing any denizen of hell that might be hiding inside Ivor's miserable house.

"Get in there, boy," James ordered, pointing towards Ivor's hovel. The dog looked at its master, then at the doorway, waited a few moments to finish marking its territory then with what seemed to be an incongruous smile on its long face, walked over to the opening. Another grunted command from James who stood nervously at the end of the leash, as far away as he could get given the length of the rope, and the dog shoved its muzzle against the rotten old door and shoved its way inside.

James let go of the leash and hefted a big stick while the rest of the men crowded in close, moving nervously forward, grasping their own assorted weapons, ready to either defend themselves from whatever hideous demon was inside the hovel or, perhaps, to run as fast as they could in the opposite direction.

Sheer weight of numbers gave the village men some confidence and they gathered in a silent semi-circle around the slippery entrance to the house, more joining them all the time as word spread throughout the village of what was happening. Some carried candles which cast a very dim light on the strange, snowy scene and Ivor's fear began to turn to pride.

The devil had come to his home this Yule. The people of Brandesburton would remember Ivor every Christmas after this, assuming they all survived the hell's fire that was sure to burst upon them any moment.

The idea made him pause but the continuing silence from inside his home lent him courage and he shoved his way to the front of the gathering, glancing at James who returned his look with a nervous shrug.

"It's your house."

Ivor nodded bravely, squaring his shoulders and hauling himself up to full height. It was his house right enough – he should be first inside.

One of the men offered him a short club and he took it with a grim nod of thanks then stepped forward to grasp the door handle. He could hear nothing from inside and his imagination conjured the most hideous demons, picturing them tearing James's poor dog apart with terrific yet silent violence.

He drew a deep breath, hefted the length of wood he'd been given and reached a hand forward to push the door open wide enough for him to follow the hound inside.

Before he could touch the iron latch though, a great black shape appeared, pushing its hellish body hard against him and, with a scream of terror Ivor fell backwards, arms flailing, onto the snow-covered grass, trying to drag himself away from the satanic presence that had hauled its carcass from his home.

The near-hysterical laughter of his fellow villagers brought him back to his senses though. It was no devil that had burst forth and attacked him; it was the dog, and it was currently doing a shit in the snow right beside him much to the amusement of the gathered locals.

James came forward, peering inside the doorway, and waved a hand dismissively.

"There's nothing there. Whatever made those hoofprints is gone; the place is empty."

He held a hand out to Ivor and hauled the old peasant back to his feet.

"Come on, I'll come in with you and make sure everything's safe. The bailiff can check the place over tomorrow, assuming he bothers his arse to visit."

The pair moved inside, the dog bounding after them happily, jumping around, tongue lolling stupidly, apparently incredibly excited to have emptied its bowels.

The hovel appeared untouched but Ivor knew better. He only owned one thing of any value – a silver spoon that had belonged to his deceased wife. He'd been thinking of selling it since he could do with the money and had no family to pass it onto anyway, but now...it was gone. Whatever demon had visited his home that December night had taken the one thing he had that was worth a coin or two.

He looked around fearfully, as if seeing the meagre furniture in his own home for the first time and James took pity on him.

"Come on, Ivor. You can stay at mine tonight. The dog will keep watch for us. He's a good lad."

The old peasant looked up gratefully and nodded his head without saying a word. It was a kind gesture and he was glad of it for he knew he didn't want to sleep in his own home where the devil had been. But he looked at the slim hunting dog and shuddered.

Even a mastiff wouldn't be any use if the devil came back for them that night.

* * *

The bailiff didn't come to Brandesburton the next day. He was based nine miles away in Beverley so, although the recent stories of the so-called devil had reached him he was too busy to make the journey on the basis of some insubstantial rumours. No-one had died and the only things taken were of little value for the most part.

Peasants' houses were easier to break into than nobles'; not that there were many of those in Brandesburton. If someone important had been robbed the bailiff might have come but petty thefts didn't interest him.

Instead, a succession of interested passers-by stopped off at Ivor's now notorious house while they went about their daily business. The old peasant was, of course, out working with his fellows, mending a fence that had blown down in a storm three nights before, but he hadn't even bothered locking the door before he left that morning. He had nothing worth stealing now, so the curious villagers were free to peer inside the open doorway although, to their credit, they were respectful and left the place as they found it.

The watchful presence of one of Ivor's neighbour's – Jeannie, a widow who was out repairing the thatch on her roof which the cursed storm had taken chunks out of – helped make sure none of the nosey visitors lingered too long around the place.

Her eyes lit up when she spotted the approach of a tall, portly friar who carried himself like a soldier rather than a clergyman.

"Brother Michael," she called, waving a hand from the top of the rickety ladder she was standing on. "You come to see the devil-house?"

The friar smiled in return. "I have. Is this it here?"

The peasant woman climbed nimbly down from her perch and walked across to join 'Brother Michael'. That was the name Father de

8

Nottingham, priest in their local church of St Mary's, had given when he'd introduced the friar to his congregation a few months earlier but it hadn't taken long for people to recognise the big man.

Friar Tuck – one of Robin Hood's trusted lieutenants. It was common knowledge the famous wolf's head and his gang had been granted pardons, so the villagers couldn't understand why Tuck was apparently hiding in Brandesburton under an assumed name. The problem was, however, the pardons granted by Sir Henry de Faucumberg, High Sheriff of Nottingham and Yorkshire, were only secular. He had no authority over the clergy. And Tuck had upset an extremely wealthy and influential clergyman in Prior John de Monte Martini of Lewes.

Tuck had been in possession of a near-priceless relic that had once belonged to the priest here in Brandesburton. He had brought it back and asked Father de Nottingham to let him stay there for a while, until Prior de Monte Martini forgot about him. Which was wishful thinking but, for now, 'Brother Michael' was safe enough, and comfortable too, since he'd brought his own considerable share of the loot Robin's gang had amassed during their hugely successful career as outlaws.

"Aye, that's old Ivor's house," Jeannie nodded, leading the friar to the sad little building and ushering him inside.

He looked around but, at first glance at least, there was nothing of any great interest. It was a regular small dwelling with one room, a firepit in the centre of the floor, a single stool for sitting on, a wooden box that probably doubled as storage and a seat for visitors, and a pallet for sleeping on.

There was little in the way of utensils or the like, and nothing ornamental or decorative whatsoever. It was a very depressing place, Tuck thought, thinking of the contrast between this and the obscenely lavish chambers Prior de Monte Martini revelled in back in Lewes.

"Why would a devil want to come here?" Jeannie wondered, gazing around at the old man's meagre belongings. The place made her own, similar, dwelling seem almost like a manor house by comparison.

Tuck shrugged. "Satan invites himself in wherever he sees an opening. It matters not to him whether a home is grand and extravagant or small and...rustic," he muttered diplomatically. "Still, what proof do we have there was any supernatural force at work here? Did anyone see it?"

It had been a dry, clear day but even so the hoofprints from the previous night were gone – trampled into mud by the gawking visitors, so Jeannie did her best to describe them to the big friar who listened intently, trying to picture them in his head. Two-toed, like the print a goat would leave behind only bigger.

"I've heard stories like this before," he admitted. "Hopefully next time the devil pays a visit I can see the thing for myself or, at the very least, the trail it leaves behind."

Jeannie nodded. "I expect a hard man like you would put up a good fight, even against Satan himself."

Tuck grinned, his small blue eyes twinkling at the compliment, and the woman excused herself so she could finish the repairs to her roof.

When she'd gone the friar moved slowly around the room, peering into the shadows and wishing he'd brought a candle from the church. Ivor had a candle beside his chair but it was almost done and Tuck knew the man would struggle for money to replace it so he left it unlit and stared at the dim floor, trying to find something – anything – that might shed light on the previous day's fearful visitor.

Eventually, just as he'd decided to give up and return to St Mary's, a robin landed on the threshold, cocking its head up at him.

"Hello, little fellow," the friar smiled, and the red-breasted bird flew back out the door, but Tuck's eyes were drawn to the spot where it had landed and he walked across, squinting down into the gloom to see it properly.

A footprint.

He knelt to inspect the mark more closely and revised his assessment – it was a hoofprint!

Whatever had made the mark must have got its foot – hoof – wet in the snow, so when it came inside Ivor's house the water had run off and turned the solid earth to mud, leaving this shallow print.

Tuck looked at it with great interest, measuring the size against his hand and noting how far into the hard-packed floor it had sunk.

Finally, head beginning to ache from straining

his eyes, he got to his feet and muttered to himself in puzzlement.

It seemed the villagers were right to be afraid – the hoofprint proved that.

He shuddered and made the sign of the cross before saying a blessing over the threshold and, with a final, preoccupied wave to Jeannie, made his way back to St Mary's. The church wasn't that big but Father de Nottingham had a small, well-appointed library and Tuck wanted to see if he could find out something about that strange hoofprint.

* * *

The library at St Mary's was a mine of information, Tuck found. Unfortunately none of it was much help in deciphering the cloven hoofprint from the peasant's house.

There were half a dozen shelves stacked with books in the fusty little windowless room, most of which were standard religious or philosophical texts with the odd historical treatise. Tuck was most intrigued – and surprised – to find ancient tomes on demonology and magic; tomes with titles like *Liber Aleph*, *De Vermis Mysteriis*, *Cultes de Goules* and one particularly loathsome volume called simply *Necronomicon* which had the most disturbing images and incantations Tuck had ever come across.

Clearly, Father Nicholas de Nottingham took an interest in the dark arts, no doubt in order to fight them more effectively. But in all these hellish texts

Tuck could find nothing of any use regarding the strange hoofprint.

There was the odd mention of such pagan monstrosities as Dionysus or the horned, piping god Pan, but Tuck couldn't accept that either of those had really visited Brandesburton.

The hoofprint he'd found simply didn't fit.

He looked down at his hand, thinking back to how he'd measured the print. It had been big enough to belong to a large animal, certainly, being about the same size as his own meaty palm. What puzzled him was the depth of it in the soft earthen floor of Ivor's hovel. Surely Pan or Dionysus would weigh enough to leave a substantially deep mark in the ground? Yet the print Tuck had found had barely left an impression.

"How are you getting on?"

Tuck looked up blearily from the text he was examining. It was written in what he assumed was German, which he couldn't read, but he was turning the pages in the hope of finding an illustration of hoofprints similar to the one he'd found on Ivor's floor.

"Ah, *Die Unaussprechlichen Kulten.* An interesting book." Father de Nottingham sat down in the empty chair next to Friar Tuck with a small smile on his lips. "I didn't know you could read German."

"I can't," Tuck replied, rubbing his eyes with his fingertips. "Not that it matters. I'm sure there's nothing of much use in any of these books, be they in German, Latin, French or English. You have an astonishing – and very strange – library, Nicholas. But I'm starting to think whatever demon is haunting the village isn't in any of your books here."

The priest nodded. He too found it difficult to believe that a devil was stalking Brandesburton with the sole intent of stealing the odd silver spoon or mouldy loaf. What need did Satan have for bread after all? He feasted on the souls of sinners didn't he? Not the crumbs left by peasants.

"What are you thinking?"

Tuck sat in silence for a moment, marshalling his thoughts.

"I'm thinking we need to find out more about this so-called devil."

Father de Nottingham nodded slowly in agreement and Tuck continued.

"We should talk to the other people that have been robbed, or any other witnesses that have seen the thing. Build up a picture of what it looks like. At least then we could go through your books with a better idea of what we're looking for."

The priest smiled, intrigued and excited at the idea of investigating the mysterious thefts; nothing like this had ever happened in Brandesburton while he'd been there.

"What are we waiting for then? I don't have to say mass for a few hours yet – let's go!"

* * *

Their first port of call was the village headman, Eustace, who'd lost an arm fighting against the

Scots in 1314. He was a clerk, and a good one at that, with a silver beard and a competent, business-like air which Tuck appreciated.

"From memory, there have been half-a-dozen of these burglaries," Eustace told them, bobbing his head thoughtfully as he stood up. "Let me just get you the notes I took. I add to them whenever something else is reported you know. Here."

He quickly looked through some documents in a drawer and drew one out which he handed to Father de Nottingham.

"It's all in there. You can hold onto it while you investigate this strange business but, please, return it when you're done. I pride myself on keeping accurate records of everything that happens in the village."

The clergymen promised to take good care of the Eustace's notes and, with waves of thanks, left the man's neat little home to visit the people listed as victims of the devil's break-ins.

The closest name on the list was Francis Baker, whose shop had been targeted at the end of November. When they reached the building Tuck examined the lock, noting its poor quality; covered in rust and with a bent latch which was almost as thin as the parchment the headman had given them. Such a shoddy fastening couldn't have kept one of the local children out, never mind Satan himself.

"You should get that repaired," Tuck told the baker as he and Father de Nottingham walked in, smiling to offset the judgemental tone of his words. "Don't want any more visits from the devil

15

do you?"

Francis looked up from kneading a heavy lump of dough, flour coating his hands and apron, and smiled when he saw who his visitors were.

"Aye, I know Brother Michael, I've got the blacksmith making me a new one. A much sturdier one." He lifted a big rolling pin and proceeded to flatten the dough expertly, working it into a near-perfect circle and Tuck found his mouth watering at the delicious smells in the room. "I've been sleeping here every night since that fiend broke in, just in case it comes back." He smiled sheepishly. "Been shoving my workbench here against the door, right enough. Don't want something like that sneaking up on me when I'm asleep!"

"Something like what?" Tuck wondered. "Did you actually see the devil? Eustace's notes say you had loaves, a ladle and," he unrolled the parchment and squinted at it before continuing, "a knife stolen."

"Aye, that's right," the baker confirmed, placing his loaf onto a baking tray beside a number of others ready for the oven. "The thing took all that and aye, I did see it. Or I should say, *them*."

Tuck was taken aback. "There was more than one of them?"

Francis nodded. "Two. One was small, one was much bigger. A demon and its imp I thought. Both of them had horns and the little one...glowing eyes it had." The man looked up at them fearfully before lifting more dough from a great bowl next to him. "I'd gone home for the night then realised I'd left my knife here so came back to get it. When

16

I got here the door was open. I thought I must have left it like that by accident so I just walked right in. It was dark but the moon was up so I could see – just – where I was going. I know this place like the back of my own hand anyway."

He stopped what he was doing and fixed Tuck with a steely gaze, daring the friar to call the truthfulness of his tale into question.

"I saw them, then. Staring at me with those glowing, red eyes. Small, much smaller than me but...the bigger one made a noise in its throat, like Satan himself growling. The atmosphere went cold, like the air had turned to ice."

He shrugged and turned back to his dough, ashamed. "I nearly soiled my hose, I was so afeared. I ran out, screaming and shouting, I don't mind admitting it." He glared back up at them, pounding the dough like it had done something to offend him. "You'd have done the same if you'd seen those horns and heard that bestial sound it made."

They thanked Francis for being so candid, bought a couple of savoury pastries from him, then moved onto the next name on Eustace's list.

Arthur of Exham, a middle-aged peasant with a horrendous skin condition hadn't seen the devil, just the hoofprints it left in the mud and snow outside his ramshackle old house. He'd been asleep – drunk – and heard nothing during the night. When he'd roused himself in the morning he'd found his last meat pie gone and the devil's tracks leading off into the woods nearby.

The clergymen carried on to the next victim on

the list, Tuck slipping Arthur a few pennies before they left to replace his stolen pie and fill his empty aleskin.

Elizabeth-atte-Gate had a more interesting tale, having seen the devil – singular this time – with her own eyes when she'd been woken up by the draught that had blown inside her small but neat home.

"Tiny it was – moved like a cat, though," she told Tuck as they sat at her surprisingly well-made little table. "I'm sure it had horns, but its eyes didn't glow like some people say. I think it had a tail though."

The friar raised an eyebrow and nodded, writing down his own notes to add to the incomplete ones Eustace had given them.

"What did it steal?"

Elizabeth clenched her fists and bit her lip in consternation, brows lowered. "My husband's citole. He died just last month, as you know, father."

De Nottingham nodded sadly. He'd presided at Elizabeth's husband's funeral.

"I'd been hanging onto it because...well, I knew I'd have to sell it to keep things going around here. I do well enough cleaning for some of the local merchants but times are hard. I couldn't bring myself to sell John's citole though, not yet...He loved to play it in the evening and I'd sing to his music...It would have fetched a good price too, I know that. But the fiend took it!"

She glared at Tuck and the big friar was glad he wasn't the thieving devil at that moment – the

18

wronged peasant woman would have ripped him apart with her bare hands.

"I chased it, the bastard. Right out the door and along the street. Funny thing was, it seemed to get even smaller when I started after it, like it was shrinking." She spat in disgust. "Fiend climbed over a fence and I had to give up the chase. Never was much good at climbing."

They blessed Elizabeth and promised to pray for the return of the stolen citole. The proud woman would probably have slapped Tuck if he'd handed her a coin so he dropped it on the floor instead, next to her sleeping pallet as he and the priest made their way out the door. She'd be glad of it without feeling like it was charity.

The rest of the victims and witnesses on the headman's list had similar tales to tell and Tuck noted everything down in his neat script. When they'd visited everyone they returned Eustace's document to him before heading back to the church. Night was drawing in and the clergymen wanted some warm food and a hearth to take the chill from their bones.

Whatever the answer was to this mystery, it would have to wait for another day.

* * *

Anne Barber and her mother, Erzsebet, who was originally from far-off Budapest, had spent a fine afternoon in their Brandesburton home, making their kissing bough which now hung proudly from the rafter. The ball of holly and bay leaves had two

19

apples stuffed inside its willow frame, and it looked beautiful with two candles burning gaily on it and a sprig of mistletoe hanging underneath.

At thirteen, Anne was excited by the kissing bough much more than she'd been in years past. Would one of the local boys want to kiss her beneath it this Christmas? She'd even taken a small cutting of the mistletoe for herself and wore it tucked inside the hem of her sleeve, hoping to attract a suitable husband.

After they finished the kissing bough and Father, home now from his barber shop, had hung it up safely so the candles wouldn't set the house alight. Her mother helped Anne bake a pie with beef, lamb, fruit and spices, which the family would eat as part of their Christmas day meal. Anne carefully marked her initials in the pastry and placed it on the hearthstone. It was an old tradition that, at midnight, the spirit double of her future husband would enter the house and mark his initials into the savoury.

For the magic to work, ideally it should be Christmas Eve when the pie was baked and left out but Anne was too excited to wait the few extra days so, when her parents had gone into their bedchamber for the night the girl lifted it from the greasy table and carefully placed it by the hearth, praying to God that William, the carpenter's son with the liquid blue eyes and unruly brown hair, would come in the night and place his initials next to her's…

Smiling, she climbed into bed and closed her eyes. Her blankets were pulled up tightly this night

– tradition stated the entrance must be left open so the spirit husband would be able to enter and mark the pastry so Anne had left the door just slightly ajar. As a result, a gentle but icy draught blew around her, and she was glad she'd placed another log on the fire before snuggling into the cosy bedding.

Her mother had reminded her to douse the candles in the kissing bough before going to bed but... it was chilly in the room and she was so cosy now, wrapped up in her thick blankets and…

Before she knew it the girl was fast asleep.

A noise broke the silence and Anne woke, trying to hold onto the dream she'd been lost in. It had been about a tall young man with brown hair and deep blue eyes. Irritably she wondered what had roused her. Then she heard it again.

Footsteps, to the side of her bed.

She came to full wakefulness and remembered the pie. Had her spirit mate come? Too frightened to roll over and face whatever was in the room she lay in silence until it became too much to bear.

Turning her head ever so slightly and as quietly as possible, she looked through hooded eyes at the centre of the room.

And screamed.

The figure that had come into their house had horns on its head and, when Anne shrieked it jumped in surprise before rushing towards the door with a strange gait, heedless to what was in its way.

"Da! Come quick – the devil's here, in our house!"

She screamed again as the figure knocked the kissing bough off the rafter onto the table below and the candles set fire to the evergreen foliage which surrounded them.

Her parents rushed from their bedchamber, wide-eyed, her father carrying a sturdy cudgel which he always kept by his side at night, but even in that short space of time the flames had taken hold of the greasy wooden table and the heat was intense in the low-ceilinged dwelling.

"Out! Get out!"

Her father pushed his wife and daughter ahead of him and the family stumbled out into the snowy night, crying and shouting for aid from their neighbours.

Of the horned demon there was no sign.

Anne, shivering with the cold and the shock of her encounter, cuddled into her mother's body, tears rolling down her cheeks.

Now she'd never know if William had signed his initials in her Christmas pie.

* * *

The entire village was humming with the news of the devil's latest exploit, as Tuck found the next morning when he went outside for his habitual daily walk.

He visited the remains of the dwelling the beast had visited, finding only a burnt out shell. The neighbours told him the family had gone to a relative's house a short way away. They also told him what had happened: how a seven-foot tall devil with red eyes had broken in during the night and cast a fireball at the young girl, Anne, who lived there.

There were slight hoof-prints in the snow roundabout, just like one at Ivor's house, and Tuck made the sign of the cross fearfully as he thanked the helpful neighbours and made his way back to St Mary's to tell Father de Nottingham of the latest events.

This devil was getting braver and more aggressive with each passing night.

By the time he reached the church again many of the local people were making their way inside. Mass wasn't normally said on weekdays, but, with it being so near to Christmas and with all the rumours of Satan stalking the village, Father de Nottingham had taken to celebrating mass most days in the lead up to the twenty-fifth of the month.

Tuck enjoyed the priest's sermons, so, with a last quick look over the notes he'd taken during the previous day's investigations, he filed inside the church with the rest of the congregation and stood near the front, as far from the doors as possible to try and escape the winter chill.

The mass began with a carol, "A Child Is Boren Amonges Man", which Tuck had written himself many years earlier when he'd first become a Franciscan. It seemed perfectly appropriate given recent events.

He'd written the words down at the start of the

festive period for Father de Nottingham who helped his choir learn the song, and now everyone joined in with the gentle melody, their voices filling the stone building.

Hand by hand we shule us take,
And joye and blisse shule we make;
For the devel of helle man hath forsake,
And Godes Son is maked our make.
A child is boren amonges man,
And in that child was no sin:
That child is God, that child is man,
And in that child oure lif bigan.

As the mass proceeded Tuck found his mind wandering to the problem at hand. The testimony of the victims differed – wildly in some cases – but there were some common themes in the majority of the accounts: the devil was small, belying the size of the prints it left; sometimes there were two of them, with one being even smaller than the other; they had horns; they walked on cloven hoofs; the bigger of the pair could make a hellish, blasphemous growl.

Ultimately, every one of the witnesses had been scared witless by their encounter with the devils and Tuck sifted through the information they'd gathered in his mind even as he went up to accept the Eucharist from Father de Nottingham.

The devil only seemed to rob easy targets – empty houses or those with the door left unlocked. Furthermore, the robberies always occurred at night, with the satanic thief targeting food as well as whatever meagre valuables it might find. Apparently it ate human food rather than human flesh which was at least somewhat reassuring.

The mass ended and, as the celebrants filed out, kneeling to pay homage to the crude but colourful nativity scene Father de Nottingham erected every year, Tuck concluded that the mystery may be deeper than anyone suspected.

He made his way back to the vestry where he found the priest, tired but happy at how the evening celebration had gone.

"Good mass. I enjoyed it." Tuck clapped the man on the back and smiled before getting straight to the point. "Our cloven-hoofed fiend burned down a house a short way from here last night. I'm thinking we should lay a trap for it before it kills someone or worse."

Father de Nottingham baulked at the suggestion, almost tripping himself as he hauled his cassock over his head. He was no man of action; the idea of coming face to face with a demon, or whatever it was that haunted their village, frightened him and with good reason. He looked at Tuck, and, seeing the confident gleam in the friar's eyes, nodded agreement with a heavy sigh. The big Franciscan was, after all, a former member of Robin Hood's band of outlaws. A hard man with martial skills enough to have been trusted as a guard for some of Christendom's most valuable relics by the likes of Prior John de Monte Martini down in Lewes.

If anyone could stand against a demon, it was Friar Tuck. Still, something seemed odd about the whole affair to the priest.

"Why are you so interested in this, Tuck?" he

asked. "This is a job for the bailiff or the reeve, not a visiting friar."

The Franciscan didn't answer immediately. He wasn't quite sure himself why this mystery had so consumed his thoughts recently, but that strange glint of light that had drawn his attention to the hoofprint in Ivor's house played on his mind. "Who knows?" he finally replied. "I just feel like something's guiding me to solve this. Someone, or some *thing* perhaps, needs our help."

Father de Nottingham shrugged in resignation. So be it.

"What do we need to do?"

"Good man!" Tuck grinned, the excitement in his eyes at the prospect of the hunt contagious. "We need a person that lives alone and I think I know who..."

* * *

"What? Are you insane Brother? I don't want no creeping devil coming in here –"

Tuck placed a couple of silver coins on old Jeannie's table and the widow broke off her rant to eye them suspiciously. It was a fair sum of money – enough to keep her in bread and ale for a while at least. And in return for what?

"You just want to stay here for the night? In the dark? In hopes that the demon that's haunting the place will break in? That's all very well, but what will the people say? I can't have two men sleeping under my roof – even clergymen!"

Father de Nottingham nodded in understanding. "Of course not, Jeannie. You can stay the night at the manse. Take a friend. I've left out meat and cheese and" – he glared at Tuck who pretended not to notice – "a jug of communion wine. It's not cheap stuff either," he grumbled.

"Have no fear for your property," Tuck reassured the woman, whose eyes had lit up at the thought of a night in the manse with good food and drink. "We'll stay on guard all through the night. I have some...experience in the arts of war. If the fiend turns up I'll defend your home with my life. But I honestly don't believe it will come to that."

Jeannie eyed the Franciscan thoughtfully. She was a good judge of character and she knew the friar could be trusted; knew too that 'Brother Michael' had probably been in more fights than anyone in Brandesburton, and won most of them too.

"You have a deal, then. May God protect you. What should I do?"

Tuck beamed, the first part of his plan falling into place.

"Come to St Mary's tonight, before sundown. With your friend, if you plan on bringing one to keep you company. We'll have your meal laid out for you and you can sleep in our beds for the night. Once you're settled Father de Nottingham and I will come here and prepare ourselves for the long night ahead of us."

The clergymen made their way out through the low doorway, waving farewell to the widow who had one final question.

"What if the devil, you know...kills you both and burns my place down, like it did to that family the other night?"

Father de Nottingham blanched at the prospect. He hadn't really thought of an outcome like that – Tuck's enthusiasm had kept his mind from such bleak thoughts.

"Have no fear, mistress," Tuck said confidently. "The devil will find me a hard man to best. But, if he manages it and brings your house down about us well, I have coin enough to pay for any repairs. I'll leave the money with your headman, Eustace, to be collected in the event of your home's untimely destruction."

Jeannie grinned and waved the men off. "God bless you then! And all his saints protect you from that horrible beast. I'll see you at the church at sunset."

* * *

Once Jeannie and her friend, a middle-aged spinster with the filthiest laugh Tuck had ever heard, were comfortable inside St Mary's manse – cups of wine in hand and trenchers filled with cheese, black bread and even a prized hen's egg between them when they were scarce at this time of year – the two clergymen bade the women goodnight and had Jeannie bolt the sturdy door securely behind them.

Tuck and Father de Nottingham might be in for a long, freezing and doubtless frightening night, but Jeannie and her friend planned on making the most of the well-stocked hearth and the communion wine.

Candles cupped in hands already beginning to turn blue and numb the men of God trudged through the slippery streets towards Jeannie's house. It was snowing gently but there was no wind to speak of and, despite the bitter cold, the men found themselves in good spirits as the sounds of families singing carols and enjoying Yule games and stories came to them through Brandesburton's locked doors and shuttered windows.

Their dim, gently flickering candles lit the sprigs of holly with their red berries symbolizing the blood of Christ, ripe as if they might burst, and the ivy that traced its way prettily around all the doors in the village. It truly seemed a magical December night as the snow fell all around them and Tuck prayed God would be with them as they sought to get to the bottom of this mystery.

Before long they reached Jeannie's house and Father de Nottingham used the key the widow had given them to unlock the door. One of the woman's neighbours opened his door to let his rangy dog out into the snow to relieve itself. The man caught sight of them and froze for a second, surprised at the sight of the hooded men entering the old woman's house but his face softened in relief when he realised who they were.

"Hail, Father," he shouted. "What's going on?"

"Nothing, James," de Nottingham replied, smiling at the harrier which, having just emptied its bowels in a steaming pile, was haring around in

29

the snow as if it had never seen the cold white stuff before. "We're just visiting. God grant you good rest this night."

Tuck shoved the priest into Jeannie's hovel and shut the door behind them to put an end to any more of James's questions. The last thing they wanted was a crowd of curious onlookers turning up to see if the devil would appear. Not much chance of that happening unless the street was deserted.

They heard James shouting at the dog to come in; his voice rose as the excited animal ignored him at first, then, when it did go back inside the house it must have trampled its own faeces into the frozen floor as they heard the villager roaring in outrage.

Finally, after some more shouting and yelping – and a muffled scolding for James from his wife – quiet settled once more on the village. Tuck unlatched the door and left it slightly ajar to make the place seem an easy, attractive target for the devils, then they heated a big stone in the fire and Father Michael placed it gingerly under the blankets to warm the bed.

At last, the clergymen settled down for the long night ahead.

"You take the first watch," Tuck suggested. "I'll get some sleep. Wake me when the candles burn down to here."

"I shall. Rest easy," Father de Nottingham nodded as Tuck made marks in the wax with his finger nail then hid the guttering candles inside a small alcove so their light wouldn't be easily seen from the street outside.

With a grunted, "Good night," the friar lay down on Jeannie's pallet which was hardly fit for a king but plump and comfortable enough for an outlaw friar, with fresh straw and a thick old blanket which was lovely and cosy now thanks to the hot stone. It was certainly better than sleeping on the forest floor, as he'd had to do many times in Barnsdale as a member of Robin Hood's gang, and the big Franciscan was soon snoring contentedly.

The night drew in and an eerie silence settled over the village which Father de Nottingham found unnerving. He brought out his old coral rosary beads which were practically worn to nothing after many long years of use, and passed the time mouthing silent prayers, his eyes fixed nervously on the slightly ajar front door. Every so often it would twitch gently in some unnoticed breeze and the drowsing priest would come fully awake with a fearful start, expecting Beelzebub himself to blast him into ashes.

Even the sounds of drunks staggering home faded at last as clouds closed in over the moon and Brandesburton changed from a friendly, welcoming village to an eerie, silently befogged netherworld that chilled Father de Nottingham's bones much worse than the cool air ever had before.

The gentle snoring from Friar Tuck and the occasional soft snuffle from the house next to them – which the priest assumed was James's dog sniffing curiously under the door – went some way to banish the loneliness Father de Nottingham felt in the near-suffocating darkness but he sighed heavily and offered a special prayer of thanks when the hidden candles spilled their wax and burnt down, at last, to Tuck's markings.

"Wake up, it's time for your watch."

Tuck groaned loudly, angrily, as the priest shook him gently awake and Father de Nottingham grimaced in fear, glancing at the open front door as the friar's muttering filled the black silence jarringly.

"Shut up, man, you'll scare anyone away with your noise!"

Groggily, the Franciscan opened his eyes and stared at the priest. Clearly Tuck had no idea where he was and, shockingly, a massive fart broke the chill air, reverberating around the hovel as the clergymen looked at one another, wide-eyed.

"In the name of Christ," de Nottingham whispered furiously, "this was all your idea! I think I'd rather face the devil himself than withstand another of those filthy blasts. Wake up will you!"

Eventually Tuck came to and poured himself a mug of wine from the skin they'd brought with them. "Get some sleep," he told Father de Nottingham. "If you hear screaming, rouse yourself. Rest assured, though, it won't be mine."

He smiled and brought out the wicked-looking club that he'd carried on his person for years. That club had protected him and even saved his life many times. It was the same club that he'd used to knock the wind out of the notorious outlaw Adam

Bell before laying the man out cold and, ultimately, joining the group that eventually became Robin Hood's fabled band of friends.

The priest nodded – pleased to have such a competent companion with him on that freezing, nerve-racking night – and settled into Jeannie's pallet which was still invitingly warm from Tuck's recent slumber, even if the stone they'd heated earlier had cooled by now.

"Wake me if you need me," he said earnestly, drawing the covers up around himself, and then was asleep almost as soon as his head rested on the linen-covered log.

"I will," Tuck smiled appreciatively, knowing Father de Nottingham had a good heart and even better intentions, even if he wouldn't be much use in a fight to the death with the devil. "I will, my friend."

* * *

Friar Tuck had spent many long nights sleeping outside in the forests of Barnsdale and elsewhere; in the dark and cold when the mists between the worlds of the living and the dead parted and the two merged into one...

For all his strength – both physical and spiritual – the clergyman was afraid. He knew demons and devils existed. He knew evil was a real force in the world and he understood that, sometimes, for His own unfathomable purpose, God didn't heed the prayers from His faithful.

So he sat in the near-pitch black, silently

offering *Pater Noster* and *Hail Mary*, but clutching his cudgel grimly, knowing his strong right arm might count for more than even the most sincere supplication this night, when the freezing moon hung portentously over the land.

He'd wrapped himself in three thick blankets but cursed the door which had to be kept open to entice any nocturnal visitors, as he could almost see the frost slipping into the little dwelling and covering him with its sparkling coat which looked so lovely but promised danger or even death for those with no flame to warm their homes.

Tuck contemplated getting up and banking the fire, even just rousing the embers in the hearth a little to take the worst of the chill from the air inside the hovel, but he knew it could mean the ruin of their plans. The place had to appear unoccupied. So he sat, hunched in the corner behind the slightly open doorway, with his woollen blankets and his cudgel and his prayers, hoping the devil showed its horned head soon.

The temperature inside the room was even and had been for a while, yet, even so, there was still the occasional thump or crack as a floorboard settled and the friar jumped involuntarily with each small noise.

He had a large cup of strong wine which he'd sat on the firepit to warm and he sipped that, trying to banish the chill as best he could, but it had cooled quickly within the wooden container so he set it aside irritably, wiggling his toes to try and keep them from becoming numb and frost-bitten.

There was a scream from somewhere not far off

and he gazed, wide-eyed, at the doorway. It was an eerie sound and he gripped his weapon even tighter, mouthing a silent prayer, but he knew it was just a fox.

Eventually, after finishing his wine, he began to feel warmer if not exactly cosy, and his head began to nod. Each time his chin touched his chest, though, he'd wake with a start and stare at the door, wondering how long he'd been asleep although it was never more than moments. Still, he knew he'd have to be vigilant or he'd be snoring alongside Father de Nottingham and all the devils of hell could rob the house without anyone stopping them.

His thoughts turned to his friends. Where was Robin Hood right now? Tuck knew his young friend had taken a position with the Sheriff of Nottingham and Yorkshire's staff but the friar had no idea what that position was. Had freedom brought Robin the happiness he craved and, indeed, deserved? What about Little John and Will Scarlet and all the other lads? Had Stephen, the bluff Hospitaller sergeant-at-arms managed to rejoin his Order?

And what about the cursed Prior John de Monte Martini away down south in Lewes? Had the man offered a reward for Tuck's capture – or death? Had he paid to repair the damage Tuck's companion had caused when they'd left the priory, burning much of the outbuildings to the ground in order to create a diversion? Did de Monte Martini's nose ache in the cold after the big friar had punched him on the night of that escape? Tuck hoped so, knowing it was most un-Christian of him but not caring.

He rubbed his hands under the blankets and listened intently then, hearing only silence – even the dog next door had ceased its curious snuffling a long while ago – Tuck decided to get up and pour himself more wine. He knew it wasn't the best idea but he had to do *something* to get his wits about him and, since it would, he guessed, soon be sunrise, it seemed like there would be no devils coming to rob them that night. What harm could another drink do?

Mug refilled, he settled back down, leaned his head back as far as he could and rolled it from side to side, stretching out the stiff neck muscles, then...he froze.

Had that small crack been his neck or had it, as he thought, come from the street outside?

There it was again!

There could be no mistake. Someone was in the street outside, and coming this way, slowly but surely.

Tuck silently shrugged the blankets off and got to his feet, glancing over at the sleeping form of Father de Nottingham. If he tried to wake the priest no doubt the man would make some noise and alert the visitor to their presence so the friar let his companion slumber.

Whoever was outside was cautious and moved near-soundlessly. There the occasional tiny snap as their feet crushed a twig but their approach was almost completely muffled by the thick snow that covered the ground.

Suddenly, the door moved back just a fraction and Tuck pressed himself against the wall, senses straining. The blood pounded in his ears and he wondered if he'd be able to hear even Satan himself mounting an attack on their benighted hovel.

The moonlight, sparse as it was, cast a shadow on the floor and Tuck stifled a gasp as the elongated, black figure cast there proved the witnesses testimony: the visitor had horns!

Not only that, another shadow appeared, cast by a second, smaller horned devil, as the door was pushed aside, wide enough for the twin demons to make their way inside Jeannie's house.

The first, and larger of the pair, made straight for the table, soundlessly lifting the shiny silver brooch that Tuck had left lying there as bait while the second figure remained by the door, close enough for the friar to touch if he'd been so inclined.

But Friar Tuck stood rooted to the spot, shocked and, yes, frightened by the appearance of the two devils. He wanted to beg the Lord's aid and grasp the crucifix he wore around his neck but was too scared to lift his hand in case the horned ones heard him and dragged him straight down to hell.

"What? Who's that?"

The silence was broken by Father de Nottingham's sleepy mumble as he sat up on Jeannie's pallet and squinted into the darkness groggily, clearly with no idea – yet – of where he was or what he was seeing.

"Run!"

Tuck shrank back, trying to press his considerable bulk into the very fabric of the wooden wall but the hoarse little voice made him pause.

It didn't *sound* like Satan, whose voice, Tuck imagined, would ring loud throughout the entire village. It didn't even sound like a minor demon.

"Hold! Stay where you are!"

The burly friar raised his own powerful voice in a cry that would have stopped most men in their tracks but the bigger of the two horned fiends burst past him, wriggling like an eel out of his way and into the street.

The dog next door had begun to bark excitedly and voices were raised from all quarters as Father de Nottingham finally got to his feet and stared around the room before his eyes finally settled on Tuck who was trying to keep hold of a little figure despite its screams and sharp teeth which sought for the friar's meaty, enclosing, hands.

"Run!" Again the bigger devil shouted from the shadows outside but the smaller imp still struggled with Tuck, pulling him out into the street despite its diminutive stature.

The taller one attacked the friar too now, raining blows down upon his arms, trying to break his grip on its fiendish companion, but Tuck was too strong and he held on grimly, shouting the *Pater Noster* as the three of them flailed around in the pitch black, freezing street.

The door in the house next to them was suddenly torn open, candlelight and barking sounds flooding the area as the devil squirmed and mewled in the clergyman's powerful grip.

"Let me go! Let me go!"

The bigger of the devils suddenly took flight, sprinting away into the night, seeming to shrink before it did so, just as one of the earlier witnesses had testified.

The dog hurtled out of its home towards Tuck, dragging its master, James, on a short length of rope behind it, barking excitedly as the man shouted questions at it as if the hound might answer back.

"What is it, boy? What d'ye see? Where is it?" Then, as their candlelight-accustomed eyes grew used to the cold, dark, gloom outside James spotted the friar struggling with the small horned devil. "Get it, lad! Get the bastard!"

The hound raced forward towards the imp, breaking free of the rope which attached it to its master, teeth bared in a furious growl, the hackles raised on its back.

Tuck brought up his foot and kicked the harrier in the ribs, sending it flying across the snow-covered road with a surprised squeal. It didn't try to return to the attack, lying panting in the snow watching the confrontation warily, but its master was outraged by the friar's assault.

"What in God's name are you doing, Brother Michael?" James roared, racing forward, fist clenched. "Why are you protecting the demon? Kill the bastard! Kill it!"

The man swung his fist towards the imp murderously, screaming for his dog to also "get it", but again, Tuck defended the still-struggling demon which he had now by the scruff of the neck.

"Leave it, man!" the friar shouted, pulling the devil aside and hammering his fist into James's jaw, dropping the villager into the snow as if he'd been hit by battering ram. "Leave it," Tuck repeated, his voice little more than a breathless grunt.

"Did you catch it? Holy Mary, mother of God, are you all right?" Father de Nottingham finally came out into the street, his eyes mostly on his companion but flickering nervously around too, wondering what had happened to the bigger demon and if it might return with a vengeance. "What is it? Why's it so small? Is it just a familiar?"

Tuck grabbed hold of the little horned figure at last, pulling it into his strong, protective embrace and fixing the furious but dazed James with a warning glare.

"No, it's not a familiar. Or Satan. Or even a demon." He breathed, shaking his head as the street filled with curious, frightened neighbours. "It's just a little girl!"

* * *

"Here. Have some." The big man in the grey robe handed her a steaming bowl of broth, which she took warily. Now divested of her devilish attire she felt small and frightened and almost naked in the presence of the two strangers but she knew better than to let them see it.

The horns were simply thin blocks of wood carved into shape and held onto her head by twine which, in the darkness, was invisible under her hair. The hoofs were, again, made from wooden blocks. They strapped to her feet with leather thongs and, although the friar said he wasn't going to try and walk in them, she herself had grown used to wearing them and she wished the man with the funny hair would give them back to her.

"I've seen mummers wearing stilts even bigger than these," he nodded, looking at the blocks closely. "But you move well in them. Here." He placed them on the floor next to her as she spooned some of the hot soup into her mouth noisily. "My name is Friar Tuck," he added, "but don't tell anyone. I'm hiding." He winked, but she just looked at him.

She broke a piece of the hard, crumbly bread that was on the table and dipped it into the broth, cramming it into her mouth, much of it dribbling down her chin, but she didn't care. It tasted wonderful and she meant to make the most of it.

"That'll warm you," Friar Tuck nodded, sitting down on the wooden box next to her with a bowl of his own. "The woman that lives here left enough in her great pot to make a hearty, warming meal for all of us. We could all be doing with it on a chilly night like this, eh?"

She'd overheard the two clergymen talking and gathered that they'd decided to spend the rest of the night here, in this house, rather than going back to the nearby priest's house and disturbing whoever was there right now.

"It's good to close the door against the frost and snow, bank the fire until it crackles brightly, and warm some food and ale now," the friar smiled at her. "Father de Nottingham and I have been sitting in the dark and cold for hours hoping to find out who you were."

Still she held her peace, nervously wondering what was going to happen to her.

"What's your name, lass?" Tuck asked, spooning some of his meal into his mouth. "This broth is really rather tasty," he continued, when she ignored him. "I'll wager you haven't tasted food like this for a while?"

Again, she ignored him, shovelling the last of the food into her mouth as if she'd not eaten a proper meal in many long weeks, which, she thought sadly, was close to the truth.

"Would you like some of my warmed ale? I'll drop some fresh snow in it so it's not too hot, or too strong for you?"

She suddenly had a feeling that this had happened before – in a dream perhaps? The sensation was overwhelming and she looked at the friar in wonder, understanding, somehow, that he'd been sent to help her.

Tuck took her silence for acquiescence and went out into the night with the mug he himself had been drinking from, taking a candle with him, he said, to make sure the snow he collected was pure white and not yellow from the neighbour's dog's piss. He scooped a handful into the mug then, shivering, made his way back inside, handing her the drink and pulling the door tight behind himself.

It was now at the coldest, darkest part of the night. She sipped the warm brew and watched as he rubbed his wet hands beside the flickering fire.

"How old are you?" he wondered, before answering his own question. "No more than five or six winters I'd say. Much too young to be going around in the dark, but, no matter – you're safe now."

He obviously expected her to grow drowsy after draining the ale mug and mopping up the last of the broth but she felt as wide-eyed and alert as if she'd just woken up. For the past few weeks – months? – she and her brother had grown accustomed to sleeping during the days and going abroad in the night, hunting for things to steal.

"Who was your companion?" The priest behind the kindly friar demanded and she shrank back from the harsh voice, while Tuck shook his head at the man.

"Don't mind him, girl. He still thinks you're a devil and he's frightened you might eat him." He winked at her and she giggled then mumbled "Aye," as Tuck offered her another bowl of broth.

"So you can speak. It's a start." He grinned again and she felt herself relaxing somewhat in the jovial clergyman's presence.

He motioned to the priest to lie down and go back to sleep and, when the scowling man did so, Tuck whispered to her. "He's a good man but he comes from a privileged background. He doesn't understand the hunger, or the fear and desperation, that makes someone steal. I, on the other hand, know all about living outside the law and doing whatever it takes to survive."

She wasn't at all sure what he meant. He was a

clergyman wasn't he? He called himself a friar and wore their grey robe so how could he know about stealing?

"Are you sleepy?" he asked her.

She shook her head and, without thinking, her eyes moved to the latch on the door.

"Don't worry, I won't hold you prisoner," Tuck smiled. "You can rest here in the warmth until morning and then we'll see what's to be done with you, all right?" He stood up and lifted something from the shelf above the pallet Father de Nottingham was resting on.

A ragdoll.

"Here. This little one's mother, Jeannie, is spending the night at the manse. Maybe you could look after her for a while?"

She took the toy eagerly, her eyes lighting up. "I've never had a dolly like this of my own before," she murmured. Still, she knew instinctively how to care for the "baby", and she happily pretended to feed it from her empty broth bowl, wiped its face clean and even scolded it for being naughty and asking for more of the food.

For a long time the friar simply watched her, a mug of warm ale in one hand and a smile on his round face.

"Who was the boy with you?"

She felt more at ease now, thanks to the friar's kindness and the ale she'd drank, so replied instantly, without thinking.

"My big brother." She giggled again as Father de Nottingham snored loudly then went back to feeding her doll.

"Won't he be cold and frightened out there on his own?" Tuck asked gently but she shook her head emphatically. "We should find him."

"Arnald knows how to take care of himself. Besides we have –"

She broke off abruptly and glared at the friar as if he'd stolen something from her.

"It's all right, little one," he soothed, smiling. "I promise not to hurt you or Arnald. I'm your friend." She still eyed him suspiciously but he leaned in close. "I'm one of Robin Hood's men," he whispered conspiratorially, glancing back at the dozing Father de Nottingham as if the man might turn them in to the law there and then. "I'm an outlaw just like you. We have to look out for one another, right? I can help you and your brother if you let me."

"Can't."

"Why not, lass?" he asked quietly. "Is your brother bad to you?"

She shook her head vehemently. "No! Never. But –"

Again, she broke off and turned away, cuddling the tatty old ragdoll tightly against her, rocking it and cooing softly as she stared into the flickering hearth. She felt frightened again and wanted nothing more than to get away from the kindly man who wanted to know so much. She'd heard the stories about Robin Hood – who hadn't? It was said his men were bloodthirsty killers!

Her eyes flickered fearfully towards the door again and she watched as the friar moved back away from her.

"We can talk more on the morrow," he said, smiling reassuringly. "When we're rested and the daylight has chased away the darkness." He lay on the floor next to the pallet the priest was sleeping on and gazed at her steadily. "Have no fears, lass – we'll make sure you and your brother are safe. In God's name, you have nothing to worry about any more."

She nodded at him but didn't reply. He couldn't make promises like that to her – he didn't know anything about her or Arnald's life.

Still, it was warm and cosy in here and her belly felt wonderfully full for a change. The snow continued to fall gently outside, the large flakes just visible through a gap in the poorly fitted shutters, and she pretended to brush the doll's hair with an invisible comb, cooing to it and rocking it gently as if it were a real babe, until the friar's snores echoed softly around the dimly lit hovel.

* * *

"Where is she?"

Tuck wiped his wet mouth drowsily, irritated to be woken from a nice dream although it fled as he tried to return to it and the freezing air in the room hit him.

"What? Where's who?" The mug in his hand clattered onto the floor and he tried to pull his grey robe in about him snugly, rolling onto his side as if he was in a nice comfy bed. It was an extremely uncomfortable position with his body on the floor and his head on Jeannie's low sleeping pallet but he stubbornly refused to come fully awake.

"The girl! She's gone."

Father de Nottingham's words slowly penetrated his consciousness and he opened one eye, squinting against the bright, cold sunshine that seemed to flood the little hovel.

"Damn it, why would she leave?" He groaned and, with a heavy sigh pushed himself to his feet, right hand on the wall to steady himself. "I promised we'd take care of her."

"I heard," the priest replied. "I also heard her stop talking when you were questioning her. As if she's afraid of something. Maybe we should just leave them alone – they seem to be doing all right on their own."

Tuck poked at the still slightly-glowing embers in the fire, blowing on them and adding a couple of dry twigs from the small pile stacked next to it. His first thought was to fill his belly with something warm and then…

What? What was he going to do? The girl and her brother were long gone, there was no chance he'd be able to track her even with the snowy ground outside.

"We can't just forget about them," he growled, finally getting a flame to flicker beneath the porridge pot which held just enough to furnish the two churchmen with a meagre but nutritious and warming meal. "They need our help."

"You're forgetting they're criminals," de Nottingham grunted. "They've caused a lot of trouble in the village, and stolen from people too. If we capture them the people might just string them up by their necks."

"No-one is killing children while I'm around," Tuck retorted angrily. "That's all they are: frightened children trying to survive the only way they know how. Not demons – children, and I promised in God's name to help them."

There wasn't much porridge left in the big cauldron and it was soon bubbling so the friar spooned it into bowls before it burned, handing one to the priest and beginning to eat the warmed oats himself, almost burning his tongue so eager was he to fill his belly.

"What time is it anyway?" he muttered between mouthfuls. "Looks like the sun's been up awhile."

There was a tap at the door and the churchmen glanced at each other before the voice of Eustace, the headman, came through the door to them.

"Father de Nottingham? Brother Michael? Are you still in there? We've come to see this devil you've captured."

Tuck groaned as a chorus of growled agreement from the people gathered in the street followed Eustace's words. He upended the bowl of porridge and allowed the last of it to slide into his mouth before dropping the bowl onto the little table and, wiping his mouth with the sleeve of his robe, opened the door and stepped outside.

"Where is it?" someone demanded and Tuck looked around at the people standing there. Dozens of them! Clearly he and Father de Nottingham had slept for much longer than they'd realised – long enough for someone to spread the news of the previous night's events and bring the villagers here

48

to see the hellish captive.

He clasped the brass pectoral cross he wore around his neck and a flash of inspiration hit him, seemingly from nowhere like a voice had spoken in his ear, and he instantly knew how they could find the girl.

"Where's James?" he demanded, not seeing Jeannie's neighbour amongst them. "The man that lives in that house there."

All eyes turned to see where he pointed and someone shouted back: "Laid up in his bed, Brother Michael. Says you hurt his leg during the night when you saved the devil from justice."

"Pah, what nonsense," Tuck shouted, waving a hand dismissively. "It was a little girl, not a devil. And she's gone." He pushed his way through the crowd, who muttered to one another about the thief's easy escape but no one was brave enough to meet the burly friar's eye and he pushed open the door to James's house, squinting inside imperiously.

His eyes soon adjusted to the gloom and he spotted the man lying on his sleeping pallet, watching him.

"Come in then, brother."

Tuck nodded gratefully and moved inside the little house, shoving the door closed behind him to keep the warmth from the fire in.

"I owe you an apology," the friar began but the bed-ridden peasant shook his head and waved the words away.

"No, you were right. It was just a child and I would have had the hound attack her, if I hadn't

done it myself first. You were right to stop me."
He smiled sheepishly. "Might have been better if
you hadn't hit me so hard though – twisted my
ankle when I fell. Can't walk today."

Tuck's mouth twisted in exasperation. "Sorry,
my old military training took over – we were all
caught up in the fear and excitement of the night,
including me."

"What can I do for you then, brother?"

Tuck nodded down at the dog lying on the floor
still eyeing him warily. "I came to ask you to bring
your dog to see if we can track the girl."

James grimaced. "I can't get out this bed but
you're welcome to take him with you," he said,
reaching down to ruffle his pet's ears. "He's a good
lad; should be able to track your girl unless she's
experienced enough to know how to hide her trail.
Just keep him on the rope." He gestured to the
leash hanging from a rusty nail on the wall by the
door. "He gets excitable and he'll run away from
you if you don't keep him in close. Stupid bastard."

Tuck nodded in gratitude then lifted the rope
and showed it to the hound. The beast jumped up
immediately, eyes shining and tail wagging hard
enough to cause a draught in the already chilly
room.

"Let him get her scent from something she
touched last night and he'll lead you right to her,"
James promised as the friar moved to lead the
excited dog out into the street where the villagers
still stood waiting to hear what was happening.
"Bring him back safely though, he's all I have!"

"Don't fret, we'll be back safe and sound before

too long." With a final wave of gratitude he closed the door behind him and once again pushed his way through the gathered villagers, back to Jeannie's house to find the ragdoll the girl had played with. Hopefully it would give the hound a scent to follow.

"Do you want me to raise the hue and cry?" Eustace asked, an irritated look on his face. "Are we going after the thieves?"

Tuck held the dog at peace for a moment. "No, you don't need to gather the law; I'll go after the girl and her brother by myself. They're no threat, but if they hear a load of men blundering about the place hunting for them we'll never see them again. Trust me," he growled, seeing Eustace was about to object. "I know what I'm doing."

The headman closed his mouth and met the friar's steely gaze but thought better of arguing.

"That's settled then," Tuck nodded, clasping Eustace by the arm. "I'll be back before nightfall."

Some of the locals, overhearing the conversation, shouted angrily.

"One fat clergyman to capture two notorious criminals? That's bollocks, Eustace, and you know it. The tithing should be after them and string the bastards up. What's an old friar going to do if they attack him?"

Tuck stopped in his tracks and glared at the speaker, a tall man in his early twenties. The tanner.

"I'm sure I can fight off a couple of children, Raymund," Tuck growled. "And you should be ashamed of yourself calling on your headman to

51

sanction the execution of a little girl and her brother. Especially at this time of year, when we should be giving aid to those less fortunate than ourselves. They need our help, not your rope."

The tanner sneered and Tuck moved to stand directly in front of him. "This old friar knows exactly how to handle himself if anyone comes looking for a fight, boy. You'd do well to remember that."

The crowd became silent, the atmosphere tense, and, to Tuck's amusement, James's dog actually growled at the young tanner as if ready to defend the friar, despite the fact he'd kicked the beast in the ribs just a few hours earlier.

Eustace intervened, placing himself between the two red-faced men. "Enough of this. Brother Michael is right. He should be given a chance to find the fugitives and, when he does we'll see what's to be done with them."

The tanner glared murderously at Tuck but the big friar had no interest in getting into a brawl with the man so he tugged on the dog's leash and entered Jeannie's hut again.

Father de Nottingham sat at the table, watching the flames in the hearth crackle and dance, a mug of ale in front of him and a contented look on his face.

Tuck found the ragdoll and held it to the harrier's nose. "Here boy. Fetch." He turned his attention to the priest. "You should get back to the church. Jeannie and her mate will be emptying your wine cellar."

De Nottingham looked up in alarm and Tuck

grinned.

"Probably eaten everything in the larder too."

"Yes. Yes, you're right, I was just waiting on you coming back." He stood and gestured at the dog. "You're going looking for the girl then."

"Aye."

"I won't offer to come with you," the priest said. "I think this is probably something you're much better at than I am, and I'd only get in your way. I would offer one piece of advice though: take your quarterstaff with you. They might be children but they're lawbreakers and our Lord himself knows what else is hiding out there in the woods..."

Tuck hadn't thought to take his staff but the priest's words made sense. He'd left the weapon back at St Mary's the night before, knowing it would be useless in a fight in the cramped confines of Jeannie's house, but it might prove useful now, even if only to lean on, so he accompanied de Nottingham back to the church.

Leaving the priest to tell the two curious women all about recent events, Tuck collected the quarterstaff, a skin of ale, a lump of cheese, a few strips of salted meat, and some bread. The hound sniffed eagerly at the little doll, which Tuck had asked Jeannie's permission to take on their hunt, before straining at the leash to head off into the trees that fringed the western edge of Brandesburton.

"I'll be back later today, or early tomorrow," he assured the priest. "The children can't have gone far. It might be an idea to buy some extra food for our evening meal. Hopefully I'll have a couple of extra mouths to feed, not to mention the dog."

Father de Nottingham waved farewell and watched, a prayer on his lips, until the grey robe became lost amongst the sparse winter foliage.

* * *

"Come on, boy, hurry up in the name of God," Tuck muttered, jerking on the dog's leash as it stopped, again, to mark its territory.

The beast did seem to have found the missing girl's scent; well, it was leading the friar after *something* he could only hope wasn't a local bitch in heat or another tree for it to piss against.

"Come on!" He tugged on the rope again and the dog, eyes shining and breath steaming from its apparently grinning mouth, ran forward, almost pulling Tuck off his feet as he stumbled through the thick, powdery snow at the beast's back.

They'd been travelling for quite a while already – it would be midday soon the Franciscan guessed, although it was hard to tell since heavy grey clouds obscured the sun, but his rumbling stomach suggested he needed a meal. He didn't want to take any of the bread or salted meat from his pack, as it would stop the hungry dog dead in its tracks again and Tuck really wanted to finish this hunt before it grew dark and the cold became deadly. But the animal seemed to have lost interest in the chase, as it stood, looking about it, apparently with no real idea where to go next.

Tuck pressed the ragdoll to the harrier's nostrils again but it sat on its haunches and gazed at him, tongue lolling to one side, breath steaming and the friar muttered an oath. Without the dog's keen senses to guide him, he'd never find the children.

A slight movement caught his eye then, a short way to the east and he peered at it. Just a robin, its red breast stark against the white snow. It flew closer, eyeing him, and he wondered if he should throw it a few crumbs; poor thing would be starving in this weather.

Before he could reach into his pack, though, it flew away and James's dog, which had also been watching it, stood up and dragged Tuck along in the same direction.

A short while later he looked around, wondering if they'd somehow circled back on themselves and returned to Brandesburton as the distinct, and welcoming, smell of wood-smoke filled his nostrils. Someone had a fire going nearby.

The hound glanced up at him, tongue lolling excitedly, and he held a finger to his lips as if the animal would understand the need for silence.

Shaking his head ruefully the friar let his own nose guide him towards the sweet fragrance and soon enough an old forester's hut became visible through the leafless trees. It had been built a long time ago from the looks of it; the roof had caved in and an old beech had dropped a massive branch onto one of the walls.

Yet the ramshackle hut seemed to be the source of the smell and, as they drew nearer, sure enough, smoke spiralled up from the rear of the building, into the trees which had grown up around it.

"Good boy." Tuck smiled, crouching down to

stroke the dog's smooth head. It licked his stubbled face affectionately and he shoved it away, keeping his eyes on the ruined building the whole time.

"What now?" he muttered, and the dog tried again to lick his face excitedly but he held it back by the scruff of the neck.

If the girl and her brother were in there he might need both hands free to catch them should they try to escape when he revealed himself. They might even attempt to fight him off; they may well be children but, cornered like this, there was a possibility they'd attempt to kill their would-be captor.

Still, the idea of leaving the dog tied to a branch here in the thick snow didn't appeal to him at all. It wouldn't take long for the cold to kill the tethered beast should anything happen to the friar and, although it was a bloody idiot of an animal, it had led him here and…

The dog, grinning, tried to kiss him again and, laughing quietly, Tuck shoved it away.

"Come on then, lad; you can come with me. If they run, you can just lead me to them again."

They moved slowly through the snow towards the hovel and Tuck watched the dog fretfully as the smell of roasting meat reached them. The animal seemed to know things were getting serious, as it walked calmly at the friar's side, eyes fixed on the low building, and Tuck relaxed a little. It was a hunting dog after all; it sensed their prey was close.

He moved slowly, not wanting to startle the children but, as he neared the front door, he suddenly spun round, staring into the sparse foliage behind him. There was nothing there but...he'd felt for just an instant as if someone, or some thing was watching from the shadows.

He ruffled the dog's ears and told himself to stop thinking about devils and demons. He'd found the fake carved wooden horns and hooves hadn't he? There was nothing to fear in this forest, other than the cold and the empty feeling in his stomach.

Still, the hairs on the back of his neck seemed to be standing up and he forced himself to ignore the feeling of being watched as he transferred his staff to his left hand, along with the dog's leash. Then he grasped the door handle, met the hound's eyes, and, with a deep breath, pushed hard.

There was a loud thump but the door remained shut.

It was locked from the inside.

Feeling rather silly, and knowing whoever was inside now knew he was coming, he trudged around to the back of the hut, where the wall was almost completely gone. The remnants held up the fallen branch, hardy moss covering both wall and tree and, warily, staff held tightly back in his right hand, Tuck glanced inside.

The heat from the small fire that crackled noisily under what remained of the roof hit him and he, momentarily, revelled in it, before the sight of the shocked little girl and boy brought him back to life with a jolt.

"It's all right, lass, it's only me: Friar Tuck. Don't worry, I'm alone." He grinned reassuringly at the girl. "Well, apart from the hound here, but he's a daft, friendly old fellow."

The children made no move to escape, just stared at him wide-eyed, and the dog whimpered, gazing at the little brown hare that was cooking slowly on the spit over the fire inside the ruined hovel.

"May we come in?"

Tuck didn't wait for an answer, he simply stepped over the remainder of the rear wall then lifted the dog over beside him.

"No! You have to go!"

"Come, now," the burly friar smiled. "Trust me – I'm a man of God, you have nothing to fear. I'm not here to arrest you, or make you do anything you don't want to do. In fact, I'm a fugitive myself. I was one of Robin Hood's men and a wicked prior is still chasing me, so you can be sure I'm no lawman. Come." He opened his pack and drew out the bread, meat and cheese packed inside. "We can share a meal together while we decide what's to be done here. I even have an egg."

The children glanced at one another, still fearful, but the boy moved forward and snatched the egg from the Franciscan's hand.

"I like these," he mumbled, "I remember having them before."

The lad lifted an old metal pot from the floor, nimbly jumped over the wrecked wall and scooped up a pile of snow. He climbed back over, placed the egg into the pot and sat the whole thing beside their fire so it began to heat.

"Isabella and I thank you for the food, but you can go now."

Tuck waved a hand and sat on the floor, the dog sitting down beside him, as close to the fire as it could manage without going up in flames. He knew the girl's name now; it was a start.

"Have some," the friar said, offering his bread to the children. "You look like you're hungry and one egg won't be near enough to fill your bellies."

"You have to go." The little boy shook his head forcefully, startling the friar and the dog. "Now. We don't want to go back with you. Get out and go away, we're happy here!"

"No we're not."

Tuck's eyes moved to Isabella who sat down and pulled her knees into her chest, sobs wracking her small frame.

"Aye, we are," the boy affirmed, glaring at Tuck. "We can take care of ourselves so...just go. Leave us alone. We're safe and warm here and we have enough to eat, even if we don't usually have any fancy hen's eggs, like yours."

"Please, Arnald," the girl whimpered, looking up, her eyes red. "I want to go with Friar Tuck. I don't like it here, and neither do you."

The boy glared from Tuck to his sister, while the friar simply stroked the dog and chewed on a piece of black bread. "She's right, Arnald, you know that. You can't stay out here in this old ruin forever."

For a while the young lad stared at the friar, as if appraising him, but at last he sighed then drew himself up decisively.

"Fine. But we have to go right now."

Isabella got to her feet and ran to Tuck, grabbing

hold of his sleeve and sniffling, while her big brother hurried into the back room which still had a roof over it and came back with a dry blanket and a little sack which must, the friar guessed, contain all their worldly possessions.

Whatever they'd managed to steal from the people of Brandesburton, in other words.

"Don't forget that," Tuck said, pointing at the old citole that lay in the far corner. "The woman you took it from would dearly like it back."

They still had a few hours of daylight left or Tuck would have insisted they spend the night in the broken down foresters hut, but he knew they'd make it to Brandesburton all right. They'd be cutting it fine and he would no doubt have to carry at least one of the children, if not both, some of the way back to the village, but, unless something unforeseen happened they'd be back at St Mary's before nightfall.

"Arnald is right," he said, lifting his staff and pulling the dog to its feet. "We should get moving. Here." He fumbled inside his grey cassock and handed something to the little girl with a grin. "I kept her warm on the way here, but she needs someone to look after her properly."

It was the ragdoll.

Isabella's eyes lit up and she hugged the toy in close, the happiness reflected in her eyes almost bringing tears to Tuck's before the boy broke in with a harsh whisper.

"Come on then, we have to go *now*!"

* * *

The children's obvious apprehension made Tuck wary as they left the ruined cabin and headed back out into the chill afternoon air. The dark grey clouds gathering overhead promised their journey back to Brandesburton would be a gloomy one.

The hound pulled Tuck out into the white blanket and he tugged hard on the rope leash, shaking his head with a smile as he struggled to keep his footing. A glance back at Isabella and her brother took the cheer from him. They looked fearfully into the trees all around them as if Satan himself lurked there and the friar felt a great sense of pity for them.

"Don't be afraid of the forest," he said. "These old trees won't hurt you and no devil or demon will come near us. I'm a man of God, after all." He grinned and pointed his great quarterstaff at the trail ahead. "God will protect us from any evil that might lurk nearby."

He turned to wink at Isabella and it was just as well he did for the expression on her face saved his life.

The girl's eyes widened in terror at the sight of something behind him and Tuck instinctively whipped his staff around, feeling it hit home, hard. His eyes followed its path and he was shocked to see a brawny youngster, at least as tall as himself, falling backwards against a tree trunk, face livid at the blow the friar had struck into his midriff.

Spinning the great weapon back gracefully, Tuck pointed the tip at the newcomer and growled.

"You stay where you are, boy. Right there, or I'll

61

shove this whole thing up your arse and out your mouth." He shifted his glare to Arnald and Isabella. "Well – who's this?"

Neither of the children replied, they simply stood, watching the newcomer fretfully, shivering as the snow grew heavier and the big flakes settled on their pitifully threadbare clothing.

"They're my servants," the big boy growled. "They do as I say, and you better let them go, friar, or I'll send you to your God in Heaven."

He pointed a finger threateningly and curled his lip at Tuck. "Go on, get out of here, back to whatever damn church you slithered out of. The children and I can look after ourselves. Isn't that right?"

The siblings shuffled closer together and shared nervous glances with one another but neither replied to the question.

"I said: isn't that right?" The boy bared his teeth and moved towards them, violence emanating from him like a wave of heat.

"Hold!" Tuck spread his legs in a defensive stance and held the quarterstaff at the ready, barring the boy's advance. "Clearly these two are terrified of you, so make no further moves or you'll see how fast I can *slither*. I was a soldier before I became a man of God."

The words stopped the lad's steps and the friar nodded in satisfaction.

"Good. Now, Arnald and Isabella are coming with me to Brandesburton. A broken-down old hovel in the middle of the forest is no place for children to be in the middle of winter. Look

62

around you, boy, it's snowing. You three don't have the skills to survive for much longer out here, especially when you go around thieving from the folk in the villages hereabouts. Either the cold, or hunger, or an angry mob will kill you before spring's green shoots sprout through the melting snow."

The burly friar slightly lowered his staff so as not to appear as menacing and met the young man's eyes.

"You're just a lad yourself." He held up a hand to stop the angry response then continued. "I can see you know how to handle yourself and you've done well taking care of the smaller ones here but you should be somewhere safe, not grubbing around in the greenwood. I've lived rough amongst the trees in winter myself." He shook his head sorrowfully. "I know how hard it is."

The boy just glared at him in silence.

"Come with us, you're more than welcome. In fact, I insist. What kind of friar would I be if I left you to freeze out here all alone? Come on." He lowered his staff completely and turned to glance back again at his young charges. "Let's get moving, all of us. There's a roaring fire, warm bread and fresh ale for us back at St Mary's."

"No!"

Tuck's eyes flicked to Isabella in annoyance, wondering why she'd suddenly changed her mind when she'd been happy to go with him not so long ago, but that wasn't why the girl had shouted.

He felt a fist hit him in the side and a gasp exploded from his mouth, more from outrage than pain and he spun, quarterstaff whipping round to batter into his assailant but the lad had already jumped back out of range.

The dog's leash had slipped free from the friar's hand and now the startled beast tore off into the trees without a backward glance.

"What's the matter with you boy?" Tuck demanded in exasperation, glaring at the young boy and rubbing his fleshy waist. "I'm here to help you, not arrest you." As he raised his hand to gesture, though, his words failed him.

His palm was slick with blood.

"You stabbed me."

His assailant nodded grimly, the blade now visible beneath his tatty old sleeve. "Those two are going to make me rich, Friar. They steal all the food and money we need and one day they'll steal something valuable and I can leave this place. Their devil disguise is perfect; the superstitious fools around here are terrified. And you think I'm going to let you just walk in here and take them from me?"

Tuck's mind whirled. The boy's dagger didn't have a very long blade and he hoped his generous layer of fat had absorbed the worst of it; still, even if nothing important had been damaged inside him, he was losing blood and they were in the middle of the forest, far from aid.

"You shouldn't have done that, Peter. He's a man of God. If he dies your soul will suffer eternal torment." Arnald shook his head at the older boy, who laughed shortly.

"God? To Hell with God. Where was God when

64

my parents died? Where was God when I was left to beg in the street, a child no older than you are? Where was God when you and I and your sister were huddled close together in the old forester's hut with nothing to our names but some pitiful old silver spoon?" Peter turned his glare back to Tuck. "Where was your God when I plunged my steel into your side, friar, eh?"

Isabella was sobbing heavily, tears streaking her filthy little face and Tuck knew he had to do something, now, before he lost all control of the situation.

Faster than anyone could ever have expected from a kindly clergyman with a stab wound, he exploded forward, ramming the quarterstaff at Peter's face. The boy barely saw the blow coming, but his youthful reflexes kicked in and he jerked his head backwards just as the weapon connected.

"Come on." Tuck gestured hurriedly at Arnald and Isabella, bidding them follow as he set off into the trees towards Brandesburton. "*Come on!*" he repeated, more forcefully, when the shocked pair didn't immediately move through the snow after him.

The commanding tone snapped them out of their reverie and Tuck nodded in relief as they came after him.

"What about Peter?" Arnald asked, wiping away snot with his sleeve.

"He'll be fine," the friar replied, glancing back over his shoulder, knuckles white on the quarterstaff. "I didn't hit him as hard as I might have done."

A groan came to them from the prone young man at their back and Tuck smiled in relief. He'd not wanted to leave Peter unconscious in the snow – it would have meant certain death for the boy – but there had been no other choice if he wanted to get the other two safely back to the village. Away from their cold-hearted and murderous leader.

"We'll need to move faster than this," Arnald muttered, skipping through the trees to take the lead. "Or Peter will catch us. He can run fast."

The sun's yellow glow was just barely visible through the heavy clouds so Tuck was able to guide them in what he felt must be the right direction back to the safety of Brandesburton but he could feel the blood from the stab wound oozing down and cooling on his hip.

If he stopped to bind it Peter might well catch up with them. And what could he use as a bandage anyway? He was already feeling the effects of the cold; he could scarcely afford to take something off to tear into a dressing.

Wordlessly, they trudged along the icy trail, treading as carefully as possible in case the slick leaves gave way or the snow had filled some hidden depression in the ground that could sprain an ankle or worse if one stumbled unwarily into it.

Suddenly, from some distance behind, a furious roar shattered what had been an eerie, almost deathly silence and Isabella began to cry again.

"It's Peter. He's coming for us."

* * *

66

After that initial roar of outrage Tuck and his young companions hadn't heard any signs of Peter pursuing them. They made no unnecessary sounds themselves either, not wanting to give away their position, and after they'd been walking for what seemed like an eternity the friar began to think they might reach Brandesburton safely after all.

His injury had grown increasingly painful and he winced with every step, knowing he wasn't doing the wound any good by continuing to walk so fast but what else could he do? Their best, indeed only option, was to make it to the village as soon as possible, before night fell and the cold took them.

Or their pursuer.

Was he after them? Or had he been too dazed by Tuck's strike to follow before the gentle snowfall had inexorably hidden their tracks through the bare trees?

The cold no longer bothered him and he thought that was a bad sign. He looked at the two children as they scurried ahead, Isabella's eyes dry now but wide and watchful, while it seemed the freezing air had at last dried the snot under Arnald's red nose.

Please, Lord, let me see these two to safety, even if it means the death of me.

"How did you two end up here anyway?" he asked, more to take all their minds off the situation than anything else. "Out here in the greenwood, at the mercy of an older lad."

"Our father left when Isabella was a baby," Arnald replied. "Don't know where he went but he never came home one night and Ma never seemed surprised. She died not long ago, and we ended up out on the street."

"Where was that?" Tuck demanded, outraged.

"Hull," the boy replied, shrugging as if there were lots of orphans and strays in the big port. He walked on in silence for a while, lost in thought, before carrying on. "We sheltered where we could – it was summer then, or we might not have made it. Even so, we were starving when Peter found us. He made sure we had a place to sleep in an old abandoned warehouse, and food to eat."

"He's not all bad then," the friar nodded.

"No," Isabella piped up, her voice stretched and thin in the cold. "But he made us steal things for him. Then one day he come back with blood on his hands and clothes and told us we had to run away. I don't know whose blood it was," she ended with a whisper, "but there was lots of it..."

"We've been hiding in the forest around Yorkshire ever since," Arnald continued. "When the cold weather came we were frightened but Peter told us we had to stay with him or..."

Tuck walked on in silence for a while then, trudging through the deep snow, not wanting to push the children any further. They were frightened enough as it was without thinking about the wild-eyed boy in the woods behind them.

Arnald suddenly turned, concern in his eyes, as Tuck slipped on a frost-covered log, gasping in pain as he dropped to one knee.

"Are you all right?"

"Aye, lad, I'm fine." The Franciscan nodded, blowing hard as he got back to his feet and threw the boy what he hoped was a reassuring smile but expected was more of an exhausted grimace. "Keep that pace up, we'll be in the warm church soon. Father de Nottingham will have a pot of hot porridge bubbling over the fire for us, and pokers in the flames to heat an ale for each of us!"

The children obviously believed him as they walked even faster, leaving him further and further behind. He knew they couldn't be far from Brandesburton though, so he ignored the dull ache in his side and the terrible weight in his legs and concentrated solely on placing one foot in front of the other.

He'd spent many months in woods just like this one. He'd become accustomed to their ways; to the rhythms of the flora and fauna that formed almost a single living organism all around them.

Perched on a branch in front of them sat a robin, and Tuck knew it was the same one that he'd seen earlier when the hound had lost the children's trail. It flew off and the friar stopped dead, setting his feet defensively and gazing around, sure the little bird's reappearance was no mere coincidence.

Suddenly, a shrill cry split the air directly beside them and a dark figure threw itself upon the friar. He brought his staff up just in time and managed to knock the attacker to the side before the knife that had been heading for his guts was able to skewer him.

Peter fell onto the slippery forest floor but was up in an instant and coming for him again.

This time Tuck wasn't fast enough and the younger man's bulk hammered into him, throwing him back, hard, into the solid trunk of a venerable old yew tree which rocked with the force, sending a small shower of frost and snowflakes down on the combatants.

Tuck had dropped his staff and was now grasping Peter's hands. The young man was like a rabid animal, throwing his body this way and that, trying to knee the friar anywhere he could and snarling through chapped lips.

The knife wound and the forced march had weakened Tuck badly and he wondered how much longer he could hold the crazed youngster at bay. He couldn't even attempt to headbutt the fool since he wouldn't stop moving long enough to present a target.

"Leave him alone, Peter, please!" Isabella stood to the side, hands clasped, tears gleaming as she stared at her erstwhile leader. "You're going to hurt him."

"I know that, you stupid little bitch, that's the plan!" the boy grunted. "The fat friar won't be the first person I've killed."

Arnald was hiding behind a fallen log, watching the struggle but making no move to help either combatant.

Whoever this young man was, Tuck thought, he had frightened the girl and her brother so badly they wouldn't raise a hand to stop him murdering their would-be saviour.

But Friar Tuck had once been a wrestler – one of the best in all England. He wasn't done just yet.

Hooking his right foot behind Peter's leg he jerked, hard, and the younger man fell backwards with a shout of alarm. Tuck leaned down to throw a punch into the lad's face but he hesitated...Peter looked so young lying there on the wet grass, his eyes wide in fear.

The fear soon reverted to fury though, and the downed youngster struck out again with his dagger, slicing into Tuck's leg.

The friar screamed in agony as the steel scraped right across his bone, opening a terrible gaping wound which was clearly visible through the hole in his breeches which the blade had torn open.

Isabella whimpered in horror and Peter pushed himself to one knee, a smile on his face.

They were lost in the depths of the forest with snow falling all around dampening any sounds that might carry to possible rescuers nearby...

He's going to kill me.

With a strength born of sheer desperation Tuck threw himself forward, landing on top of Peter. Ignoring the burning pain in his side and his leg he held the boy down by the neck, pushed himself up so his legs were in the air, and brought both his knees down into Peter's midriff as hard as he could.

He was a heavy man and the boy gasped in agony, the breath blasted from him. The knife fell from his hand onto the ground but Tuck knew he had to finish it now. He squeezed, the muscles in his thick arms cording like ropes. Peter's eyes bulged and he tried furiously to break free from the Franciscan's vice-like grip but no matter how he shoved and twisted his body he simply didn't have the strength to move the burly friar.

"God forgive me," Tuck sobbed, tears blurring his vision as he felt the life fade from the young man beneath him.

The two children remained where they were, Isabella still crying and shaking her head in shock while Arnald simply looked on in shock.

"You killed him."

Tuck relaxed but remained kneeling over Peter's body. "Aye."

He moved his hand to make the sign of the cross but stopped even before the bloody palm reached his forehead and he slumped down, staring sightlessly into the muddy snow.

For a time none of them moved and the friar was content to stay that way. The loss of blood from his wounds, combined with the exhaustion and cold made him want to rest here, to just curl up into a ball and sleep.

Warmth seemed to flow through him and he closed his eyes, giving in to the numbness that promised to ease his pain and guilt.

* * *

"What are we going to do?" Isabella whispered, staring at the unmoving friar lying in the mud and blood-stained snow.

Arnald shrugged. "We need to get warm before night falls or we'll die too. I wish we could go back to the forester's hut, but I don't think we'd make it before it becomes too dark to see and we lose our way..." He nodded decisively and squeezed his sister's hand reassuringly. "Come on, we need a

72

fire – let's gather some dry wood."

"What about him?" The girl gestured at Tuck. "Will he be all right lying there? Shouldn't we cover him up?"

"With what? We have nothing..."

Arnald followed the direction of his sister's gaze and blanched. Peter didn't need his clothes any more.

"All right," he muttered, shivering and pulling away from Isabella. "You find some dry twigs and sticks for the fire then."

She nodded agreement and moved off to look under the nearest evergreens for the much-needed kindling while her brother stooped over Peter's corpse.

The bigger boy was clearly dead – eyes staring into the sky unblinking, skin already beginning to take on a strange pallor – yet, even so, Arnald was terrified his 'friend' would grab hold of him if he tried to touch him.

"Hurry up," Isabella hissed. "The friar will be getting cold."

Sighing heavily, Arnald steeled himself and began to remove Peter's clothing, starting with the heavy cloak. It was hard work and, once he'd finished the young boy was glad of the exercise for he no longer felt the cold. In fact he was sweating! He'd found a flint and steel in one of the dead boy's pockets too which should make lighting a fire much easier.

Every piece of clothing Peter had been wearing was now draped over Tuck's prone figure, apart from the cloak which Arnald placed around his sister's shoulders once they'd built a fire. Isabella sat next to the friar, sharing their body heat, while her big brother attempted to make a spark with the flint.

The yew tree offered some protection from the snow which had picked up again, its green needles and ripe red berries keeping the worst of the white flakes from their makeshift campsite. But Arnald's attempts at lighting the fire proved fruitless. He'd managed to get a spark a few times but it had flared and died before setting the kindling to burning and, eventually, close to tears, the boy had given up and hunkered down beside his sister and Tuck.

Night was drawing in fast.

"Soon be Christmas Day," Isabella whispered, trying to sound cheerful, before her eyes closed and she dozed off, the snow whirling around them in the failing light.

Arnald fought sleep for as long as he could, terrified at the thought of lying in the dark next to the naked corpse of his murdered companion but, eventually, he too shut his eyes and the forest took them all into its embrace.

* * *

It was the burning sensation in his leg that did it.

It penetrated his consciousness and, with a groan, he opened his eyes

"Ow, in God's name, that hurts!"

"Peace, Brother Tuck," Father de Nottingham, a concerned look on his face, appeared at the bedside holding a cup. "You have nasty wounds in your side and your leg. I've cleaned and dressed them, but you must rest. Here, drink this, it'll help take the chill from your bones."

Tuck allowed the priest to tip the liquid into his mouth, slowly and, realising it was slightly warmed, strong ale, sipped at it greedily before lying his head back down and sighing contentedly.

"Where are the children?" he asked.

"In the next room, under a thick blanket, sleeping, safe. They told us what happened with the older boy – they saved your life by lying down beside you under their cloaks. Fear not, the villagers lost any idea of making them pay for their thefts when they saw the three of you lying near death under that tree. Any longer out there and you'd all be dead. In truth, I have no idea how you survived – given what you went through, you should be in God's arms already."

"Like..."

"As I said," Father de Nottingham broke in. "Arnald and Isabella told us everything that happened. You did what you could. You've saved two vulnerable children from certain death out there in the forest."

"I killed the lad, though. He was little more than a child himself! I've done some things in my time, Nicholas, but..." Tuck shook his head sorrowfully. "I've never throttled a young man like that before."

The priest looked away, gathering his thoughts, then replied. "I've never been in a fight in my whole life. If it had been I who had gone looking for Arnald and his sister I would be dead by now.

The big lad, Peter was it? He'd have killed me and then what? The two children would have been left out there with him. Eventually the cold or the law would have got them. From what they said you simply defended yourself against a young man who was intent on murdering you. In the morning I'll hear your confession, but… for me, you acted in the only way you could, and our Lord will know it."

He patted the friar's blanket and stood up. "Rest now, my friend. God brought you back to us – it's truly a Christmas miracle!"

Tuck smiled as he dozed off. Aye, a miracle. They were all safe and warm in Brandesburton.

All except Peter.

* * *

The bell in St Mary's tolled two mornings later – Christmas Day.

Friar Tuck was able to get up and attend mass with the aid of a crutch that James brought for him. He discovered that James's dog had made its way back to Brandesburton when Peter had initially attacked Tuck and the beast had slipped its leash. The villager realised something was wrong when Tuck hadn't appeared a short while later, so he'd sent word to Eustace who organised a search party.

The hound had been able to pick up Tuck and the children's trail at first, although it lost it after a while and the searchers feared they would never find the missing friar. Then, apparently, the dog had chased after a bird and the villagers found

Tuck and the children huddled all together, snow beginning to settle on the cloaks that covered them.

Thankfully they'd only been a short distance from the village so it didn't take long for the men to carry them all back to the warmth and safety of St Mary's.

"And to think, the first time I saw that dog of yours, I kicked it halfway across the street." Tuck shook his head ruefully at James. "It saved my life. Remind me to visit the butcher and buy it the biggest bone in his shop."

He smiled thoughtfully then, wondering what tasty morsels birds liked best at this time of year...

When Father Nicholas had finished mass some of the villagers filed out to return to their homes for their Christmas meal. Many of the poorer families remained in the church, where the priest always provided them with food and drink on this day.

The men rearranged the pews and carried in tables and casks of ale and wassail while the women set about cooking the meat from the animals slaughtered at Martinmas.

The children – and some of the adults – played raucous games like Snap-dragon or tug of war. Arnald and Isabella watched shyly at first, until some of the local youngsters grabbed them by the hands and hauled them into the fun, demanding to hear all about their adventures as the Christmas Devils.

Snow fell heavily outside and the wind howled and whistled through gaps in the shutters but

Father de Nottingham ordered the fire to be banked and the chill didn't penetrate the sturdy old stone walls which held so many happy revellers, pleased to spend a day indoors. A day when they didn't have to work but, instead, enjoyed one another's company and gave thanks to God for their good fortune.

"Wes hail!"

Tuck raised his mug of spiced cider and smiled warmly at the priest. "Drink hail!" he responded, emptying half the contents of the mug into his mouth.

"What will happen to them now?" the friar asked, as they watched Arnald and Isabella happily playing with the rest of the children as if they hadn't a care in all the world. "Where will they go?"

Father de Nottingham smiled reassuringly. "Jeannie has offered to take them in. Eustace promised to make sure she gets money to feed and clothe them until they're old enough to contribute themselves. The fact they returned some of the things they'd stolen – like Elizabeth's citole and Ivor's silver spoon – made it easier for people to forgive them. I'm not sure if the family whose house went up in flames felt so charitable but...the villagers will muck in and help them rebuild once the weather's better."

The friar nodded in relief. "The people of Brandesburton have proven themselves to be true Christians. I'm glad I came here to stay for a while."

De Nottingham shrugged. "What did you think

would happen? It's Christmas!"

Isabella ran over to them, her eyes shining and her teeth bright in her grubby face. "Tuck, come and join in with us. We're going to play Hoodman's Blind."

The friar laughed and ruffled the little girl's hair. "Look at the wound in my leg lass. I can barely stand up, never mind chase about the room with my hood over my face. Go on with you."

She hurried off again, a whirlwind of joyous, youthful energy and Father de Nottingham clasped his Franciscan friend by the arm.

"See? Those two wouldn't be here today if it wasn't for you. Peter had been taken over by Satan – he was the true Christmas Devil. Who knows what other crimes he would have dragged Arnald and Isabella into as time went on? You've given them a chance in life. And Jeannie will be glad of their company around her house. She's been lonely since her man died last summer."

Tuck said nothing for a time. It felt strange to be given advice by someone else – normally he was the wise one doling out words of guidance to Robin Hood or one of the other outlaws like this. But he greatly appreciated the priest's opinion and he knew it was true, even if Peter's dying face would haunt his dreams for a long time to come.

"Come on." Father de Nottingham grinned and pulled the friar over towards one of the heavily laden tables, almost forgetting Tuck's reliance on the crutch. "Let's get some of that pie the women have just brought out. Today should be a happy day."

"You're right." The big Franciscan nodded, raising his wassail mug and smiling thankfully at his friend as they moved amongst the happy villagers towards the food.

The Christmas pie was huge. Oval-shaped, like a crib and with a little pastry baby Jesus set on top. The women had filled it with meat and spices and everyone cheered at the sight of it being carried out and set onto one of the tables.

Tuck beamed – truly this was Christ's day.

With no warning the great front doors were thrown open, a chill wind blowing through the nave into the hall and the revellers became silent, turning as one to see what was happening.

"Where are they? Where are the devils that set alight to my house? Is that them? Little bastards!"

"Aye, that's them, Erzsebet. The dirty thieves."

"What do you think you're doing?" Father de Nottingham demanded, placing himself in front of the four newcomers. "You watch your language Erzsebet Barber – this is a house of God."

Isabella looked across to Tuck, eyes wide in fear. This was the family whose house burned down when she and Arnald had robbed it, and they were out for bloody justice now. The presence of the vindictive tanner, Raymund only made the situation even more volatile.

Tuck smiled reassuringly at the girl, and her brother who had moved to stand protectively by his little sister, but he felt a sinking sensation in the pit of his stomach as he hobbled across to join the priest.

"Do you not know what day it is?" he

demanded, glaring at the barber's Hungarian wife. She was a large woman, liked well enough by her fellow villagers but, in the name of Christ, she had a temper if anyone tried to cross her.

"I care not what the day is. Those two destroyed my house," Erzsebet said in her strangely accented voice. "They are criminals, and yet here they are, feasting and enjoying the day, while my family has no home to go to because of them!"

Raymund, the tanner, pushed his face in front of Tuck's, the whites of his eyes showing red, suggesting the man was already drunk.

"We're here to arrest them," he spat. "And you better not try and stop us, friar, or else. You're nothing in this village. Your Robin isn't here to help you now."

Tuck blinked in surprise – how…?

Then he realised what the tanner meant and he lowered his brows irritably. Despite the awful wound in his leg and the fact he was recovering from near-death, he was sure he could take the tanner down without the help of his infamous friend. But it was Christmas Day; he'd already killed one young man this festive season and the idea of beating up another was quite distasteful.

Raymund took the friar's downcast expression as a sign of fear and pulled himself up as tall as he could, pressing his forehead into Tuck's.

"Get out the way, old man. We're taking those two with us. The bailiff will deal with them next time he visits and no doubt they'll hang for their crimes."

"No!" Isabella cried, tears filling her eyes as she

dragged her brother by the hand to hide behind Friar Tuck. "It was an accident, we didn't mean to set your house on fire. Peter made us steal; we didn't want to do it. We're sorry!"

Raymund turned his malevolent gaze on the terrified girl and curled his lip. "You're a pair of filthy thieves," he grunted. "Criminals. Like this one here." He looked again at Tuck. "Aye, d'ye think we're all fools in Brandesburton, 'Brother Michael'? I know fine who you are, so you'd be best not getting in our way or you'll be swinging from a rope too, beside your little friends here..."

The tanner's head suddenly rocked back and he went down in a heap as the fist connected with his nose in a bloody spray.

Everyone in the room shouted and the place exploded in a welter of fury and, unsurprisingly, laughter, as the people crowded round, hoping to see some entertainment as the tanner struggled to get back to his feet.

"Enough!" Father de Nottingham roared, raising his arms like Moses himself and staring at everyone until quiet was restored. "There will be no more violence in God's house. Not this day, or any other."

James, whose dog had helped Tuck so well over the past couple of days, glared down at Raymund. It was James who had pushed past Friar Tuck aside and punched the tanner, and now the widow, Jeannie, came to stand by his side, facing down Erzsebet and her husband while their daughter Anne hung back, looking as if she wished the ground would swallow her.

"They're just children," Jeannie ground out. "They were forced to steal and live a miserable life out in the forest. How would you like it if something happened to you and your man, Erzsebet, and Anne had to fend for herself? Would you want people to help her? Or string her up by the neck for taking a crust to fill her empty belly?"

Her barb had clearly hit home and now the peasant Ivor, whose silver spoon had been restored to him that day, piped up.

"Come on, it's Christmas! Today is a day for celebrating and making merry. Join us."

The tanner looked murderously at James but the Barbers seemed somewhat mollified by the reaction of the revellers and Tuck knew it wouldn't take much to end the hostility.

"Join us," he repeated. "Your house is already being rebuilt and I'll personally pay to replace whatever you lost in the fire." He grinned at the family, his eyes twinkling. "Think of it as a Christmas gift."

James had disappeared into the crowd but now he returned with a brimming mug of warmed ale and handed it sheepishly to Raymund who scowled, but took it nonetheless and went off to down the contents on his own near the table stacked with food.

"Are we all right, then?" Father de Nottingham demanded, daring anyone to disagree with a frosty look at the Barbers. "Good. Let's eat!"

He smiled in relief and all attention turned back to the big Christmas pie which sat so invitingly on the long table by the back wall.

"Brother Michael? Would you like the honour?"

One of the ladies handed Tuck a spoon as everyone gathered around and, smiling, he used it to cut into the pie. Carefully, he dropped the portion onto a wooden trencher which he gave to Isabella, who watched, wide-eyed, her mouth watering.

"You get first taste, lass," he said, kindly. "And you get to make a wish too. Here, go on, try it."

Isabella, flushing at being the centre of attention, hesitantly took the piece of pie from the friar and used her fingers to scoop some into her mouth. A huge smile spread across her small face and she crammed more in, mumbling, "It's delicious," between bites, as everyone cheered. "Here, Arnald, try some."

"Don't forget to make a wish, but don't tell anyone what it is, or it won't come true." Tuck winked at her as everyone gathered around noisily, bowls and trenchers held out for their own slice of the great savoury.

"I won't." She grinned, and ran off with her brother, crumbs and sweetmeats spilling from their mouths, to join the other children who were starting yet another noisy game.

"What d'you think she wished for?" Father de Nottingham wondered, taking a long pull from his wassail cup and watching Isabella skip away.

Tuck shrugged. "The same thing we all wish for today, I expect. Peace and happiness. I pray she and her brother find it." He raised his own mug and held it out to the priest with a smile.

"Merry Christmas, Nicholas. Merry Christmas

one and all!"

THE END

And a very Merry Christmas to you, dear reader!

Author's Note

I love Christmas, always have, even though I'm not religious. It's a magical time of year, when we can spend long hours with loved ones, doing nice things and escaping the drudgery of everyday life, right? Well, things were the same back in the Middle Ages. They too looked forward to their days off work, giving gifts to one another, playing games and drinking themselves senseless!

They also sang songs (many of them bawdy) and the earliest English carol we have evidence for, *A Child is Boren Amonges Man*, which I mention in the story, genuinely was written by a Franciscan friar and dates back to sometime before 1350. Could it have been the "real" Tuck that penned it? I'd like to think so.

The other little traditions – like placing a pie on the hearthstone in the hope a spirit would come in and mark his initials in it, or the kissing bough – were real too. Mostly throwbacks to pagan or Viking times, they were updated for a Christian population although the Church frowned upon most of those old practices.

They didn't have fir trees in their houses back then but they did use holly, ivy, mistletoe and other evergreens, along with candles and the yule log to brighten the place. Let's be honest, winter must have been a gloomy and grim time for the commoners in those days. Freezing cold, even indoors with no double-glazing or central heating; food scarce; and of course, it would have been extremely dark, both inside and outside.

That, no doubt, played a part in the fearful superstitions of the people. Holly and ivy weren't just to brighten the place up – they were believed to have the power to deter witches. And it was thought that the dead returned during the festive period to check up on the world they'd left behind. Families would even set a meal for the spirits before going out to mass on Christmas Day.

In an environment like that, you can imagine how the villagers would have reacted if hoof-prints had started appearing in the snow overnight and belongings went missing...

If you're interested in finding out more, I'd recommend Sophie Jackson's lovely little book, *The Medieval Christmas*, which I found really helpful when writing this novella.

I hope you've had a great year and are now sitting with a glass of your favourite tipple, Slade, Wham! and Wizzard playing loudly somewhere in the background. Actually, all those old songs which are trotted out every year were one of the reasons I decided to write this novella. Hopefully reading *Friar Tuck and the Christmas Devil* each December will become a tradition for millions of readers all around the world for generations to come, just like Noddy Holder roaring "It's Christmas!" every five minutes on the radio or TV. Yes, even in my house, although I much prefer Jethro Tull's "Ring Out Solstice Bells".

Please look out for my fourth and final Forest

Lord novel in 2016. After that's published I'll be starting a brand new historical fiction series.

Now – get the mince pies and the booze out and...*Wes hail!*

Steven A. McKay,
Old Kilpatrick,
9 September 2015

If you enjoyed *Friar Tuck and The Christmas Devil* please leave a review wherever you can. Good reviews are the lifeblood of self-published authors, so, if you can, take a few moments to let others know what you thought of the book.
Thank you!

If you'd like a FREE short story take a moment to sign up for my mailing list. VIP subscribers will get exclusive access to giveaways, competitions, info on new releases and other freebies.
Just click the link below to sign up. As a thank you, you will be able to download my brand new short story "The Escape", starring Little John.

https://stevenamckay.wordpress.com/mailing-list/

Otherwise, to find out what's happening with the author and any forthcoming books, point your browser to:

www.facebook.com/RobinHoodNovel

http://stevenamckay.wordpress.com/

THANK YOU FOR READING!

Printed in Poland
by Amazon Fulfillment
Poland Sp. z o.o., Wrocław